Death in the Vineyard

Calvin Hill

Published by Calvin Hill, 2024.

This is a work of fiction. Similarities to real people, places, or events are entirely coincidental.

DEATH IN THE VINEYARD

First edition. October 23, 2024.

Copyright © 2024 Calvin Hill.

ISBN: 979-8227539274

Written by Calvin Hill.

Death in the Vineyard
A vineyard owner is found dead among the vines, and the detective must navigate family feuds and a bitter wine industry rivalry to solve the crime.

When renowned vineyard owner Victor Castello is found dead among the rows of his prized vines, the tranquil beauty of the Castello family estate is shattered. Called in to investigate, Detective Emma Cross must navigate a world where family feuds run deep, and the stakes of success in the wine industry are brutally high. As she delves into the Castello family's troubled past and its bitter rivalry with neighbouring vineyard magnate Luca Rossi, Emma uncovers a tangled web of hidden affairs, dark secrets, and ruthless ambition.

With each family member holding a potential motive—and the discovery of illicit business dealings, poison, and a mysterious last vintage—the vineyard begins to feel like a labyrinth of deceit. As tensions rise, Emma races against time to unearth the truth before the murderer strikes again, exposing how far someone is willing to go to protect a legacy stained by lies.

In Death in the Vineyard, the beauty of the rolling vineyards masks a sinister undercurrent, where jealousy, betrayal, and power struggles ferment into deadly consequences.

Part 1: The Vine's Shadow
Chapter 1: The Morning Fog

The fog clung low to the vineyard like a shroud, wrapping its tendrils around each row of vines and turning the land into a sea of mist. To Marco, it was a typical autumn morning at Castello Vineyards—cool, quiet, and heavy with the smell of earth. He walked along the familiar paths, his boots sinking into the damp soil as he made his rounds before the day's work began. The workers wouldn't arrive for another hour or so, but Marco liked to be the first one there, alone with the vines and the solitude of the land.

This was his father's land. It had always been. As far back as Marco could remember, the Castello family had lived, worked, and bled here. Victor Castello had built the estate into one of the most respected vineyards in the region, producing some of the finest wines Italy had to offer. But as Marco trudged through the fog, something felt different today. The air felt heavier, as though the vines themselves were holding their breath.

Marco stopped for a moment, staring out at the endless rows of grapevines that disappeared into the thick mist. His mind wandered, thinking of the meeting he had with his father the night before, the one that had left a sour taste in his mouth. It wasn't unusual for him and Victor to argue, but this one had felt different, more final. His father's stubbornness had always been the source of their friction, and last night had been no exception. They had clashed over the future of the vineyard, as they so often did.

Sighing, Marco continued down the path, his breath visible in the chill morning air. He made his way toward the eastern end of the vineyard, where the vines had just finished yielding this season's crop. Harvest had been good this year, though Marco had noticed that the workers had seemed more tired, more restless, as if something unseen weighed on them.

As he passed the old oak tree that stood at the edge of the vineyard, something caught his eye. A shape—dark, crumpled, and out of place—lay sprawled among the vines. For a moment, Marco thought it might be one of the vineyard dogs that roamed the estate, but as he moved closer, dread settled in his gut. The shape wasn't moving. And it was too large to be a dog.

His steps quickened, the sound of his boots squelching through the mud. The closer he got, the more he could make out—clothing, a body lying unnaturally still in the damp earth. His heart raced, a flood of fear rising in his chest as he recognized the figure.

"Papa?"

Victor Castello lay face down in the soil, his arms limp at his sides, his head turned at an odd angle. The fog clung to his still form, making it seem as though the earth itself had swallowed him whole. For a moment, Marco froze, unable to process what he was seeing. His father, the unshakable, formidable Victor Castello, lay motionless before him.

Marco dropped to his knees, the ground cold and wet beneath him. His hands shook as he reached out to touch his father's shoulder, his fingers brushing the rough fabric of Victor's jacket. It felt wrong—unnaturally still, like touching stone. With a sharp intake of breath, Marco turned his father's body over.

Victor's face was pale, his eyes half-open and glazed over, staring blankly at the sky. His lips were parted slightly, as if he'd been trying to speak but never had the chance. There was no sign of a struggle, no blood, no visible wounds. But there was something in the way his father's body lay, something unnatural in his stillness that sent a wave of nausea through Marco.

"Papa!" Marco's voice broke, the sound echoing through the vineyard. He shook his father's shoulder harder, as if willing him to wake up, to snap out of whatever spell had claimed him. But there was no response, only the silence of the fog and the soft rustling of the vines in the wind.

Time seemed to slow as Marco knelt there, his mind a whirlwind of disbelief and horror. This couldn't be real. His father was indestructible, larger than life. Victor Castello didn't just die—not like this, not alone among the vines. But the cold, stiff body beneath his hands told him otherwise.

He didn't know how long he knelt there, frozen in shock, before he heard footsteps behind him. Marco turned his head slowly, still dazed, to see Alessandro, one of the vineyard workers, walking up the path toward him. Alessandro had been with the Castello family for years, a steady presence on the vineyard, and his eyes widened in horror as he took in the scene.

"Signor Marco…" Alessandro's voice was shaky as he approached, stopping short when he saw Victor's body. "Is he…?"

Marco could only nod, his throat tight. He couldn't bring himself to speak, couldn't find the words to describe what he was feeling. Alessandro, pale and shaken, knelt beside him, his eyes fixed on the lifeless form of the man they had both worked under for so long.

"We need to call someone," Alessandro said, his voice low and urgent. "The doctor, the authorities…someone needs to know."

Marco nodded again, his mind still struggling to catch up with the reality of the situation. He fumbled in his pocket for his phone, his fingers trembling as he dialled the number for the local doctor. The call felt surreal, like something out of a nightmare he couldn't wake up from. The vineyard's doctor, Dr. Rossi, answered on the second ring, his voice crisp and professional.

"Dr. Rossi, it's Marco Castello," Marco managed to say, his voice hoarse. "I—I need you to come to the vineyard. My father…he's dead."

There was a brief pause on the other end of the line, and Marco could hear the doctor's intake of breath.

"I'll be there right away," Dr. Rossi said, his tone serious.

Marco hung up and stared at the phone in his hand, his heart pounding in his chest. It felt impossible that just a few hours ago, his father had been alive, still dictating orders, still making plans for the vineyard's future. And now, he was gone, his body cold and still among the vines he had tended to for decades.

Alessandro remained quiet beside him, his face pale and drawn. Marco could see the shock in the man's eyes, the same disbelief that he felt. They sat in silence for a few moments, the fog curling around them like a ghostly presence. Somewhere in the distance, a bird called out, its cry sharp and lonely in the stillness.

"What do you think happened?" Alessandro asked quietly, his voice barely more than a whisper.

Marco shook his head. "I don't know. He was fine last night. We had...we had a meeting. He didn't say anything about feeling unwell."

Alessandro looked down at Victor's body, his brow furrowed. "It doesn't look natural. I mean, he's just lying there, like he collapsed."

Marco's throat tightened. He didn't want to think about it, didn't want to consider the possibility that something more than just old age had claimed his father. But as he looked at Victor's lifeless face, the stillness in his limbs, a nagging suspicion crept into his mind.

Could this have been something more? Something...sinister?

The thought was too much to bear, and Marco pushed it aside. He needed to wait for Dr. Rossi, for the authorities, for someone to tell him what had happened. Until then, all he could do was sit there, the weight of the fog pressing down on him, and try to comprehend a world where his father no longer existed.

Minutes passed, though they felt like hours, before Marco heard the sound of a car approaching. Dr. Rossi's silver sedan appeared through the mist, pulling up along the dirt path near the oak tree. The doctor, a wiry man in his late fifties, stepped out of the car, his expression grave as he approached Marco and Alessandro.

Without a word, Dr. Rossi knelt beside Victor's body, his hands moving with practiced efficiency as he checked for any signs of life. After a few moments, he shook his head and stood up, wiping his hands on his handkerchief.

"He's gone," the doctor said quietly. "It looks like he's been dead for a few hours. Maybe a heart attack, but we won't know for sure until we can do an autopsy."

Marco stared at the doctor, his mind spinning. A heart attack. It was a simple explanation, one that made sense, but somehow it didn't feel right. Not with the way his father had been acting lately, the stress, the arguments, the tension in the air.

As Dr. Rossi made arrangements for Victor's body to be taken away, Marco stood in silence, his eyes fixed on the vineyard that stretched out before him. The fog still lingered, thick and heavy, obscuring the rows of vines like a veil.

Chapter 2: The Arrival

Detective Emma Cross stepped out of her car and into the cool morning air, her boots sinking slightly into the soft earth as she surveyed the scene. The mist still clung to the vineyard like a grey blanket, thick and heavy, making it hard to see beyond the first few rows of vines. Everything was quiet except for the soft rustling of the leaves and the distant hum of the wind as it passed through the hills. It was almost peaceful.

Almost.

The scene felt unreal, even to someone like Emma, who had seen her fair share of death over the years. The Castello Vineyard was beautiful, sprawling out for acres in every direction, its vines heavy with grapes waiting to be harvested. The air was crisp with the faint scent of fermentation from the nearby winery, and the landscape felt more like a painting than the setting of a violent crime. But just beyond the peaceful exterior, death had visited.

She exhaled deeply, her breath visible in the cold. She could feel the tension in the air—thick, almost tangible, as if the earth itself was holding its breath. Somewhere ahead, a man lay dead among the vines. Victor Castello. The name carried weight, not just in this part of Italy but internationally. He wasn't just a vineyard owner; he was a force in the wine industry, respected by many and feared by some.

Victor Castello dead. It didn't quite seem real.

Emma ran her hand over her short, dark hair, already beginning to feel the familiar knot of tension form in her stomach. She'd been called early that morning, told there was a body—no signs of foul play, not yet—but given the prominence of the deceased, she was asked to make her way to the scene. Nothing was official yet. There was no full-scale investigation, no police lights flashing, no crime scene tape.

Not yet.

As she walked up the gravel path toward the vineyard, her eyes scanned the rows of vines, neatly lined up like soldiers, as if their order and tranquillity could somehow mask the horror that had happened here. The vineyard was old, generations old, and carried with it a sense of history, of things long past but never forgotten. The soil beneath her feet was rich with stories, and today, it had added another.

Ahead, she could make out a few figures standing in the fog—two men, their shapes blurred by the mist. One of them was Marco Castello, the victim's eldest son. She'd spoken briefly with him on the phone earlier, his voice flat and cold, barely able to explain what had happened. The other man, she assumed, was a worker from the vineyard, though she hadn't gotten his name. They stood together, silent, waiting for someone to come and give them answers. Or maybe waiting for something they couldn't quite articulate.

Emma approached slowly, her pace deliberate. She didn't want to rush this. There would be enough of that later. For now, it was about observation—taking in the scene, reading the landscape, and sensing the unspoken tension. As she got closer, Marco turned toward her, his face pale and drawn. He was tall, in his early forties, with the same dark, rugged features his father had been known for. His eyes were red, either from lack of sleep or something worse.

"Detective Cross?" Marco asked, his voice tight with barely suppressed emotion.

Emma nodded, giving him a brief, professional smile. "Yes. You must be Marco. I'm sorry for your loss."

He nodded stiffly, as if acknowledging the formality of her words but unable to process them. His gaze shifted toward the vines, where his father's body still lay, covered with a plain white sheet. Emma followed his eyes and saw the still form beneath the fabric, the edges of Victor's shoes just visible. She could almost hear the story the vines were telling—of a man who had given his life to them, and who now lay among them, lifeless.

"This way," Marco said, his voice flat. He turned, leading her toward the body, his movements mechanical, as if he were trying to get through the motions without really processing what was happening.

Emma followed in silence, her eyes scanning the ground, noting the small, seemingly insignificant details that would form the basis of any eventual investigation: the footprints in the dirt, the way the vines around Victor's body were slightly trampled, the direction in which the sheet was pulled. No police had arrived yet, and Emma knew she'd have to be careful about what she saw. There was no official crime scene, but that didn't mean the answers weren't already here, waiting to be uncovered.

As they reached the body, Marco stopped, his back straight but his hands trembling slightly at his sides. He stood for a moment, staring down at the covered form of his father. Emma could feel the weight of his grief, a silent pressure that hung between them. She said nothing, giving him the space he needed to process it, however long that might take.

"The doctor came," Marco said quietly, his voice rough. "He said it was probably a heart attack. My father... he wasn't a young man. But..." His voice trailed off, and he swallowed hard.

Emma waited. She could feel the hesitation in his words, the unspoken doubt that hung in the air like a thread waiting to be pulled.

"But you don't believe it," she finished for him, her voice gentle.

Marco looked up at her, his dark eyes hard and searching. "I don't know what I believe. My father... he was stubborn. He wouldn't have just died out here, like this. Not without a reason."

Emma nodded. It was something she'd heard many times before—grief clouding judgment, refusing to accept the natural order of things. But there was something in Marco's voice, a crack in his certainty that made her pause. She had learned long ago not to dismiss those cracks. They often revealed more than people realized.

She crouched down next to the body, careful not to disturb the ground around it. Gently, she pulled back the sheet just enough to see Victor's face. His skin was pale, his eyes half-closed, his expression frozen in something close to surprise. No obvious injuries. No blood. But something about the way his body lay among the vines felt wrong. It wasn't the peaceful repose of a man who had quietly passed away. There was a tension there, a stiffness that told her Victor hadn't simply fallen to the ground. He had collapsed.

Still, there were no signs of violence. No reason to think this was anything other than what the doctor had said: a heart attack, a natural death. But even as Emma tried to settle into that explanation, a nagging doubt began to take root in her mind. Why was Marco so certain that this wasn't just a tragic accident?

"I've been arguing with him for months," Marco said suddenly, his voice tight. "About the vineyard, about the future. He wasn't well... but he wouldn't listen. He kept pushing himself, kept acting like nothing was wrong."

Emma stood up, letting the sheet fall back into place. She turned to Marco, her gaze steady. "What do you think happened?"

Marco hesitated, glancing back at his father's body. "I don't know. Maybe it was his heart. Maybe it wasn't. But my father had enemies, Detective Cross. In the business. And in the family. If there's more to this..."

He didn't finish, but Emma could hear the unspoken words hanging between them. *If there's more to this, I need to know.*

Emma straightened, taking a deep breath. "For now, we'll wait for the official cause of death. There's no indication of foul play, but I'll keep an open mind."

Marco nodded, but his expression remained strained, as if he were holding something back. "The rest of the family will be here soon. My mother, my siblings. It won't be easy."

"I understand," Emma said, though she suspected she didn't yet grasp the full extent of what he meant. Family dynamics could be as complex as any crime, and in a family like the Castellos, where the stakes were high, the tensions were likely to run deep.

As Emma looked out over the vineyard, the fog still thick in the distance, she felt the weight of what was to come. For now, no investigation had officially begun. But soon, very soon, there would be questions. And as much as Marco might want answers, Emma had a feeling that not everyone in the Castello family would be so eager for the truth to come to light.

The vineyard was peaceful now, but it was only a matter of time before the calm broke—and the real storm began.

Chapter 3: Blood on the Grapes

The sun had started to burn away the early morning fog by the time Detective Emma Cross returned to the vineyard, flanked by a small team of forensic specialists and officers. What had once been a scene shrouded in mist now felt more exposed under the sharp, clear light of day. The sprawling vineyard seemed different—colder, somehow, as if the beauty of the place had been tarnished by the events of the morning.

The quiet calm of the vineyard was replaced with the low murmur of voices, the crackle of radios, and the occasional barked order as the investigation slowly came to life. Emma stood at the edge of the rows, watching the technicians work with methodical precision, documenting every footprint, every piece of disturbed earth, and every vine that had been trampled in the immediate area around Victor Castello's body.

The body had been removed earlier, transported to the medical examiner for a formal autopsy, but Emma had asked for detailed photographs and the results of the preliminary examination as soon as possible. Something about the scene—about Victor's death—felt off, even though it was too early to say why.

She was reviewing notes when one of the forensic officers, a young woman named Gina, approached, her gloves stained with the dirt of the vineyard.

"Detective Cross?" Gina said, a hint of hesitation in her voice. "There's something you might want to see. I think it's... unusual."

Emma looked up, her interest piqued. "Show me."

Gina led her back toward where Victor's body had been found, near the eastern edge of the vineyard. The vines there were heavy with grapes, their dark purple skins almost black in the bright sunlight. To an untrained eye, it might have looked like nothing more than a patch of disturbed soil, but Emma could see the subtle signs—the trampled vines, the crushed clusters of grapes beneath where Victor's body had fallen.

Gina crouched down, pointing to a section of the ground where a fine layer of red, almost burgundy-coloured juice had stained the earth.

"At first, we thought this was just crushed grapes," Gina said, her eyes narrowing as she pointed at the ground. "But it's more than that. There's a pattern in the stains here, and when we tested some of the samples... well, it's not just grape juice."

Emma knelt beside her, her eyes following Gina's finger as she pointed out the stains. Now that she was looking closer, she could see what Gina meant—beneath the rich juice of the grapes, a darker, more sinister liquid had soaked into the ground. Blood.

"What else did you find?" Emma asked, her voice calm despite the rising sense of unease.

"There are strange markings on the vines themselves," Gina said, standing up and leading Emma over to one of the nearby plants. "Here."

Emma bent closer to the vine, and her brow furrowed. The tendrils and leaves near where Victor had been found had strange marks on them—faint but noticeable—almost like burns. Some leaves had shrivelled, their edges blackened, and the vine itself had small, discoloured patches that didn't look natural.

She ran a gloved hand over the vine, tracing the faint markings. "Any idea what could have caused this?"

Gina shook her head. "We're not sure yet. But it doesn't look like anything we've seen from typical agricultural chemicals or pesticides. We're running more tests, but I've never seen vines react like this before."

Emma stood up, glancing around the scene again. The crushed grapes, the blood, the burned vines—it all felt disconnected, like pieces of a puzzle that didn't quite fit together. There was no obvious sign of a struggle, no weapon, no immediate evidence of foul play, but something about the scene told her that Victor's death was more than just an unfortunate accident.

Her phone buzzed in her pocket, breaking her concentration. She pulled it out and saw a message from the medical examiner, Dr. Rossi. He had already begun his preliminary assessment of Victor's body and had sent over his early findings.

Emma opened the message and skimmed through the report. As she read, her stomach tightened.

The autopsy was far from complete, but Dr. Rossi had noted several unusual details. While Victor's death could have been attributed to heart failure, the cause wasn't entirely clear. There were signs of internal trauma, but no visible external injuries—nothing to suggest that he had been struck or attacked. More disturbingly, strange marks had been found on Victor's skin, particularly on his arms and chest. The marks were faint but distinct, almost like chemical burns or abrasions caused by something that wasn't immediately identifiable.

Emma read the line again, her mind turning over the possibilities. Could those marks be connected to the strange discoloration on the vines? Could Victor have come into contact with something—some substance or chemical—that had affected both him and the plants?

She tapped out a quick reply to Dr. Rossi, asking him to focus on the marks and run tests to determine what could have caused them. In the meantime, she needed to talk to the family. Victor's sudden death was one thing, but these new details raised too many questions to ignore.

As Emma approached the Castello estate, she could see the house looming at the top of the hill, its elegant facade standing in stark contrast to the quiet chaos below. The Castello family was inside, waiting, and Emma knew that the next conversation she had with them would be critical. Family dynamics were always complex, and the Castello family was no different.

When she reached the front steps, she was greeted by Marco Castello, his face still drawn with grief but laced with something else—impatience, perhaps, or frustration.

"Detective," Marco said, his voice clipped. "Any news?"

Emma nodded, keeping her expression neutral. "We've just begun the investigation, Mr. Castello. There are a few details we're looking into that are... unusual."

"Unusual?" Marco's eyes narrowed. "What do you mean?"

"There are markings on your father's body," Emma explained carefully. "And on some of the vines around where he was found. We're running tests to determine what might have caused them, but at this point, we can't rule out the possibility that something else was at play."

Marco's expression shifted—grief mixing with confusion and anger. "What are you saying? That my father didn't just die of a heart attack?"

"I'm saying that we need to consider every possibility," Emma replied, her voice steady. "Right now, we don't have enough information to make any conclusions. But we'll know more soon."

Marco clenched his jaw, his hands tightening into fists at his sides. "If you think someone did this to him—if you think someone killed my father—I want to know."

Emma met his gaze. "I understand. But I need to ask you some more questions, Marco. I need to understand your father's recent behaviour, any enemies he might have had, anything unusual leading up to his death."

Marco hesitated, glancing back at the house. "We've had our share of problems. The vineyard business is competitive—brutal, even. My father was a hard man to deal with. But I didn't think..."

He trailed off, and Emma could see the uncertainty in his eyes. The cracks in his certainty were beginning to show.

"Did your father have any dealings with dangerous people? Anyone who might have had a grudge against him?" Emma pressed.

Marco shook his head, though he didn't look entirely convinced. "He had rivals. Plenty of them. But no one I can think of who would do something like this."

Emma filed that away, knowing she'd need to look into those rivals—especially Luca Rossi, the head of the neighbouring vineyard, whose rivalry with Victor was well-known. But there was something else, something more personal in Marco's hesitation.

She glanced back toward the vineyard, where the vines were still thick with grapes, some of them stained with blood and secrets.

"Marco, did your father have any plans for the vineyard—any changes he was considering that the rest of the family didn't agree with?" Emma asked.

Marco's eyes darkened. "There were always plans. My father was always pushing for something new, always making decisions on his own. He didn't care who he upset along the way."

Emma nodded. There it was—another thread to pull, another piece of the puzzle.

As the investigation continued to unfold, Emma couldn't shake the feeling that Victor Castello's death wasn't just about the vineyard or business rivalries. There was something else here, something buried deep beneath the surface of the family's carefully cultivated image. And the blood on the grapes was only the beginning.

Chapter 4: The Family Legacy

Detective Emma Cross took a deep breath before stepping through the heavy wooden doors of the Castello family estate. The house itself was a sprawling, old-world villa perched on the hillside, overlooking the expansive vineyard below. Its grand arches and stone walls were built to impress, a reminder of the Castello family's long-standing success in the wine industry. Yet today, the air inside felt heavy with tension, as if the grief and suspicion had sunk into the very walls of the house.

Emma's footsteps echoed through the marble entryway as she was led by a housekeeper into the main sitting room, where the Castello family waited. She had already met Marco briefly at the vineyard, but now she would face the rest of them. The Castello family was a cornerstone of the local wine community, and each member, she suspected, played a role in shaping Victor's empire—and perhaps in his death.

The sitting room was a blend of classic elegance and modern comfort, filled with antique furniture and family portraits, the soft hum of an old grandfather clock ticking in the background. The atmosphere, however, was anything but calm. The family members sat scattered around the room, their faces etched with grief, but something else lingered there—something darker. Emma had seen it before in families touched by tragedy: the unresolved conflicts, the unspoken accusations, and the subtle undercurrents of resentment that no amount of wealth or success could smooth over.

Victor Castello's widow, Isabela, sat on a plush armchair by the large bay window, her back straight and her hands resting in her lap, clasped tightly together. She was a striking woman, even in her late fifties—her long, dark hair streaked with silver, her posture dignified despite the circumstances. She looked like a woman who had spent her life standing by her husband's side, playing the role of the dutiful wife, but there was a hardness to her gaze, a controlled composure that made Emma wonder what lay beneath it.

Next to her stood Marco, his expression as tense as it had been earlier at the vineyard. His tall, broad frame seemed too large for the room, his arms crossed over his chest as he paced near the fireplace. His movements were restless, the anger simmering just beneath the surface.

Across from Marco sat his younger brother, Alessandro. Slighter and shorter than Marco, Alessandro had the look of someone who had always been in the shadow of others. His casual clothes contrasted with the tension in the room, but his eyes flicked nervously between his mother and brother, as though unsure of where he stood in all this.

Then there was Adriana, Victor's only daughter. She sat apart from the others on a low velvet sofa, her legs crossed elegantly and her arms draped over the back of the couch. With her sharp features and piercing green eyes, she exuded a cool confidence that set her apart. She seemed less affected by the grief that hung over the room, her gaze focused on Emma with an air of curiosity—and something close to amusement.

Emma cleared her throat, drawing the family's attention. "Thank you for meeting with me. I know this is a difficult time for all of you, but I have some questions that may help us understand what happened to your husband and father."

Isabela nodded, though her face remained expressionless. "Of course, Detective Cross. We want to know what happened to Victor. This... situation is unbearable."

Emma glanced around the room, noting the tension in each of their postures, the way they avoided looking at one another. It was as though Victor's death had broken open cracks in the family dynamic that had long been hidden beneath the surface.

She decided to start with the matriarch. "Mrs. Castello, I understand this is a difficult question, but did your husband have any recent health issues? Anything that might suggest his death was due to natural causes?"

Isabela's mouth tightened slightly. "Victor was not in the best of health. He was getting older, of course, and he had some heart issues. But nothing so serious that we expected this. He had always been strong. Too strong for his own good, perhaps."

Emma nodded, filing that away. "And his stress levels? Running such a large operation like Castello Vineyards must have been demanding."

At this, Marco let out a bitter laugh. "Stress? My father thrived on stress. He was always working, always pushing us harder. He didn't know how to stop."

Isabela's eyes flashed with irritation as she glanced at Marco. "Your father built this business with his bare hands, Marco. Everything we have is because of him."

Marco's jaw tightened, but he said nothing. Emma could sense the long-standing tension between mother and son, and the way it had only deepened in the wake of Victor's death.

Emma turned her attention to Alessandro. "What about you, Alessandro? How involved were you in the vineyard's day-to-day operations?"

Alessandro looked uncomfortable under her scrutiny. "I... I help with some of the logistics. I've always been more interested in the financial side of things. My father and Marco handled most of the winemaking. They liked being in the thick of it."

There was a hint of resentment in Alessandro's voice, as though he had always been on the periphery, watching his father and older brother take the reins of the business while he was left behind.

"And how was your relationship with your father?" Emma asked.

Alessandro shrugged, avoiding his mother's gaze. "It was fine. I mean, we didn't always see eye to eye, but who does? He was tough, but he was fair... most of the time."

Emma shifted her gaze to Adriana, who had remained silent through most of the conversation, her cool expression giving little away. "And you, Adriana? Were you involved in the vineyard?"

Adriana smiled, a small, knowing smile that didn't quite reach her eyes. "Not in the way my brothers were, no. I've always had other interests. But that didn't mean I didn't care about the vineyard. My father and I had... our differences, but I respected what he built."

Emma raised an eyebrow, catching the hint of something unspoken. "Differences? What kind of differences?"

Adriana leaned back, crossing her arms over her chest. "Let's just say my father had very specific ideas about what each of us should be doing with our lives. He wasn't exactly flexible when it came to my choices."

Emma could feel the undercurrent of resentment in Adriana's words, the way she distanced herself from the family legacy, from the vineyard. It was clear that each of Victor's children had a complicated relationship with their father—and with each other.

Isabela, sensing the shift in conversation, spoke up again. "Detective, what exactly are you suggesting? That Victor's death was not an accident?"

Emma chose her words carefully. "At this point, we're exploring every possibility. There are some unusual aspects to the scene where your husband was found, and we're waiting for more information from the autopsy. I just need to understand the dynamics here—any tensions or conflicts Victor might have been involved in, either within the family or outside it."

Isabela's eyes narrowed slightly. "Conflicts? Victor had no more conflicts than any man in his position would have. Running a successful vineyard in this industry isn't easy, Detective. There are always challenges, always competition. But nothing... nothing that would lead to this."

Marco scoffed. "Come on, Mother. You know how much pressure he was under. The Rossi family has been trying to undermine us for years. The competition in the wine business is brutal. It's not just about making good wine—it's about winning. And my father was obsessed with winning."

Emma noted the sharpness in Marco's tone, the way his words were laced with anger and frustration. She filed that away as well.

Before she could ask another question, the door to the sitting room opened, and an elderly man entered, leaning heavily on a cane. His lined face and sharp eyes immediately told Emma who he was: Vittorio Castello, Victor's older brother and a man who had once been deeply involved in the vineyard before stepping back in recent years.

"Detective," Vittorio said, his voice gravelly but commanding. "I hear you're asking about my brother."

Emma stood and nodded respectfully. "Yes, Mr. Castello. I'm trying to gather as much information as I can to understand what happened."

Vittorio gave her a long, considering look before turning to the rest of the family, his expression hardening. "My brother's death was no accident. I knew something like this was coming. He made too many enemies—both inside and outside this family."

The room fell into a tense silence at his words, and Emma felt the weight of what had just been said settle over the room like a heavy fog. Inside and outside this family.

Emma watched the faces of the Castellos closely, noting how none of them seemed particularly shocked by Vittorio's statement. Each of them had their own agendas, their own resentments, and their own relationship with the man who had controlled their lives for so long.

As she looked around the room, Emma knew that the truth about Victor Castello's death wasn't just buried in the vineyard. It was buried deep within the hearts of the people sitting in this very room—each of them harbouring their own secrets, their own motivations.

And one of them, she suspected, knew exactly what had happened to Victor Castello.

Chapter 5: Rivalries Run Deep

Detective Emma Cross sat at a small wooden table on the terrace of a local café, her notebook open in front of her as she sipped from a cup of strong espresso. The late morning sun had fully burned away the lingering fog from the vineyard, and now the rolling hills stretched out in front of her in golden green splendour, rows of vines neatly lined up as far as the eye could see.

Yet, the picturesque landscape masked a much darker story. Victor Castello's death was just the tip of the iceberg, and Emma could already feel the weight of something larger brewing beneath the surface. Every family, every successful business had its share of secrets, but something about this case felt especially tangled. And the more she pulled at the threads, the more she realized that Victor's death wasn't just about family tensions—it was about power and control over a vast, fiercely competitive industry.

She closed her notebook and looked up as a figure approached her table. Luca Rossi. Emma had made it a priority to meet him after the Castellos' comments about long-standing tensions between the two families. The Rossi family owned the neighbouring vineyard, and if there was one thing Emma had learned in her years of investigative work, it was that rivalries in industries like this often ran deeper than blood.

Luca walked with the confident stride of a man accustomed to getting his way, but there was something restrained about his movements, as if he carried the weight of unspoken tension on his shoulders. He was around the same age as Victor had been, though his sharp eyes gave the impression of someone constantly evaluating the world around him.

"Detective Cross," Luca greeted her in a voice that was deep and smooth, offering her a polite but tight smile as he extended his hand. "I hear you've been asking questions about Victor."

Emma shook his hand, noting the firmness of his grip. "Thank you for meeting with me, Mr. Rossi. I understand your family and the Castello family have a history. I'd like to know more about that."

Luca took a seat across from her, leaning back slightly in his chair as if trying to assess just how much he should say. He didn't strike Emma as the kind of man who was easily intimidated or flustered, but she could sense a guardedness in him—one that spoke volumes.

"Our families go back a long way," Luca began, his tone measured. "My vineyard, Rossi Estate, has been around for generations, just like Castello Vineyards. We were neighbours, yes, but we were never friends."

Emma raised an eyebrow. "Rivals, then?"

A small, bitter laugh escaped Luca's lips. "You could say that. The Castello family always wanted to be the best. Victor was obsessed with it—his wine winning awards, his brand becoming the face of Italian viticulture. He didn't care how many people he stepped on to get there, including my family."

Emma took a sip of her coffee, keeping her expression neutral. "What kind of conflict are we talking about? Business competition or something more personal?"

"Both," Luca said, his voice hardening slightly. "Victor and I—well, let's just say we never saw eye to eye. My father and his father started the feud, and by the time Victor and I took over, it had escalated into something far more bitter. He undercut us at every opportunity, always looking for ways to poach our customers, our contracts. He even tried to buy out one of our key suppliers behind my back."

Emma nodded slowly, her pen poised over her notebook. "That's pretty cutthroat."

Luca's jaw tightened. "This business is cutthroat, Detective. The wine industry may look glamorous from the outside, but it's a vicious game. You don't get to the top by playing nice."

Emma could hear the anger simmering beneath his words, and it struck her that whatever had gone on between Victor and Luca, it wasn't just business for him—it was personal. There was a deep, festering resentment there, and while Emma hadn't yet concluded that Victor's death was the result of foul play, she couldn't ignore the fact that the rivalry between the two families could have easily turned deadly.

"Was there any recent incident between you and Victor?" Emma asked, probing further. "Anything that might have escalated the tension between your families?"

Luca hesitated for a moment, his eyes narrowing as if weighing how much he wanted to reveal. Finally, he leaned forward slightly, his voice lowering. "About six months ago, Victor made a play for a piece of land that borders both our properties. It's prime vineyard land, perfect for growing high-quality grapes. He knew I wanted it—I'd been negotiating with the owner for months—but Victor went behind my back and outbid me."

Emma frowned. "Did that cause any confrontation between you two?"

"It caused more than that," Luca said, his voice tight with barely suppressed anger. "I confronted him. I told him that land should've been mine—that he had no right to swoop in at the last minute. But Victor didn't care. To him, it was just business. He was always like that—cold, calculating. He saw the vineyard as his kingdom, and he wouldn't let anyone challenge him."

Emma could see the frustration in Luca's eyes, the bitterness that had clearly built up over years of competition. But there was something else in his tone—a sense of finality, as if the land deal had been the last straw in an already strained relationship.

"Did you threaten him?" Emma asked, keeping her voice calm but direct.

Luca's eyes flicked up to meet hers, and for a moment, his expression was unreadable. Then he leaned back in his chair, his face hardening. "I'm not a fool, Detective. I wasn't going to start a war over a piece of land, even though it was the last straw for me. But did I threaten him? No. I told him what I thought of him, sure, but I wasn't going to risk everything my family has built on revenge."

Emma made a note of Luca's words, but she couldn't shake the feeling that there was more beneath the surface. Rivalries like this—long-standing, deeply rooted in personal and business grievances—had a way of festering until they became dangerous. And while Luca claimed he hadn't threatened Victor, Emma couldn't rule out the possibility that tensions between the two men had reached a boiling point.

"Did anyone else in your family have any dealings with Victor?" Emma asked, switching gears slightly. "Any personal conflicts that might have caused problems?"

Luca shrugged. "My son, Antonio, has been more involved in the business recently, but he didn't have the same history with Victor that I did. Antonio's young—he's ambitious, but he knows the rules of the game."

"And your workers?" Emma pressed. "Anyone who might have had reason to cross paths with Victor?"

Luca's eyes darkened slightly. "Victor didn't just make enemies in his family, Detective. He wasn't particularly well-liked in the community, either. He treated his workers like they were disposable. Paid them poorly, worked them to the bone. Meanwhile, we treat our workers like family. That's why we've always had loyal people on our side. If you're looking for someone who might have had it out for Victor, you might want to start with his own people."

Emma nodded, considering Luca's words. The Castello family had already hinted at tensions within the vineyard's workforce, and if

Victor had mistreated his employees, that could have created even more potential enemies.

"Thank you for your time, Mr. Rossi," Emma said, standing up and offering her hand. "I appreciate your insight."

Luca shook her hand, his expression serious. "Just know this, Detective—whatever happened to Victor, it wasn't me or my family. We had our differences, but I wouldn't stoop that low. The Rossi name has survived too long to be dragged into something like this."

Emma gave him a small nod and watched as Luca walked away, his shoulders stiff with tension. As she sat back down, her mind raced with the new information. Luca had provided a glimpse into the darker side of the wine industry, where competition was fierce, and grudges could last for generations.

Victor Castello had clearly been a man who made enemies, both within his family and beyond it. Whether his death had been the result of a natural cause or something more sinister, Emma knew that the rivalry between the Castello and Rossi families was a crucial piece of the puzzle.

But as she stared out over the vineyard, the sun glinting off the rows of vines, she couldn't shake the feeling that there was still more to uncover. Someone—whether in the Castello family, the Rossi family, or the vineyard itself—knew more than they were letting on.

And whoever it was, Emma was determined to find them.

Chapter 6: Bitter Harvest

The sun was dipping below the horizon, casting long shadows across the vineyard as Detective Emma Cross made her way up the gravel path that led to the Rossi Estate. The air was cooler now, with the warmth of the day giving way to the crispness of early evening. The sprawling rows of vines, once vibrant with the light of the sun, now seemed to stretch on endlessly, their darkened shapes moving gently in the breeze.

Emma had requested another meeting with Luca Rossi, and this time, the atmosphere felt different. Her previous conversation with him had been informative but guarded—Luca had been polite enough, but there had been a distinct sense that he was holding something back. Today, she was determined to get a deeper understanding of the feud that had plagued the Castello and Rossi families for generations. It was more than just business rivalry; it was personal, and old wounds like that rarely healed cleanly.

The Rossi estate was every bit as grand as the Castello villa, though its style was more modern, with sleek stonework and large glass windows that reflected the setting sun. A sharp contrast to the traditional, almost old-world charm of the Castello property. As Emma approached, she could see Luca waiting for her at the entrance, his hands in his pockets, his posture rigid. He looked less composed than the last time she had seen him—more on edge.

"Detective Cross," Luca greeted her, his voice clipped. He motioned for her to follow him, leading her around the side of the estate and toward a shaded terrace that overlooked the vineyard. The view was stunning, but Emma could feel the weight of the tension between them, thickening the air.

"Thank you for meeting with me again," Emma said as they reached the terrace. Luca didn't respond immediately, instead standing by the stone railing, staring out over his vineyard. His silence, coupled with the darkening sky, gave the moment a heavy, almost foreboding quality.

Finally, Luca turned to her, his expression hard. "I thought we'd covered everything, Detective. I told you what you needed to know about my family's rivalry with the Castellos."

Emma met his gaze, unwavering. "You told me some of it, yes. But not all of it. I need to understand how deep this feud really goes. It's clear that there's more history between your families than you let on during our first meeting."

Luca sighed, rubbing a hand over his face as if the weight of the past was suddenly too much to bear. "It goes back longer than you might think," he said, his voice quieter now, more resigned. "Our families—Rossi and Castello—we've been at each other's throats for generations."

He gestured toward the vineyard, as if the land itself held the memories of every bitter moment. "This land has always been fought over. My grandfather told me stories about how it used to belong to the same family—long before the Rossis and Castellos arrived. But then there was a split, a disagreement over how the land should be used, and it was divided. Half of it went to the Rossi family, half to the Castello family. Ever since then, there's been nothing but bad blood."

Emma leaned against the stone railing, listening intently. "What started the feud?"

Luca's jaw tightened as he gazed out over the vineyard, his eyes dark with old memories. "Money. Power. Pride. The usual things. My grandfather accused Victor's grandfather of sabotaging one of our harvests—ruining a crop that would have made us a fortune. Victor's grandfather swore it wasn't him, but no one believed him. From that moment on, the feud began. Each generation tried to outdo the last—buying more land, growing better grapes, making more expensive wine. It became an obsession."

Emma frowned, sensing that there was more to the story than just business rivalry. "But that can't be all of it. Rivalries like this don't last for generations unless there's something deeper driving it."

Luca's eyes narrowed, and for a moment, Emma saw something flicker across his face—something darker, more personal. "There's always more, Detective. My father and Victor's father hated each other. It wasn't just about the vineyard anymore—it was about legacy, about who would be remembered as the better family. They pushed each other, and in the process, they dragged us all into it. I grew up hearing nothing but stories about how we had to beat the Castellos, how we had to be better."

He clenched his fists, his voice thick with bitterness. "And then there was Victor. Always so smug, always so sure of himself. He acted like he owned this whole valley, like the rest of us were just playing in his shadow. He didn't care who he hurt, as long as he came out on top."

Emma's mind raced as she took in Luca's words. The feud between the families was more than just a series of business disagreements—it had become a multi-generational grudge, passed down like a curse, poisoning every interaction between the Rossis and the Castellos.

"But did it ever get violent?" Emma asked, watching Luca closely for any signs of evasion.

Luca's eyes met hers, sharp and unyielding. "Not physically, no. Not between me and Victor, at least. But words can cut deeper than any blade. We had plenty of arguments, plenty of threats, but neither of us ever crossed that line."

Emma raised an eyebrow. "But the workers? The employees on both sides? They must have gotten caught in the middle of this."

Luca's expression hardened. "The workers knew where their loyalties were supposed to lie. But yeah, there were... incidents. Fights between our men and theirs. Sabotage, even. Some of Victor's people weren't above messing with our equipment, our shipments. And, of course, we had to respond. It was tit for tat for years. The police got involved a few times, but nothing ever came of it."

Emma felt a chill run down her spine as she thought about the long-standing hostilities, simmering just below the surface for decades.

Feuds like this rarely stayed clean. Even if Luca hadn't physically harmed Victor, the chances that someone in the Rossi camp might have taken matters into their own hands weren't far-fetched.

Luca stepped away from the railing, pacing slightly as if restless with the weight of his own history. "But things escalated more recently," he continued. "Victor's ambitions grew. It wasn't enough for him to run his vineyard—he wanted to control the entire market. He started working with distributors who used to be loyal to us, pushing us out. When he bought that piece of land last year, the one that borders both our properties, that was the final insult."

Emma remembered Marco mentioning the land deal, how it had infuriated both sides. "Why was that piece of land so important?"

Luca's face darkened. "That land would have given us the perfect conditions for growing a new variety of grapes—something that could have elevated our wines to another level. Victor knew that, and he swooped in at the last minute to buy it out from under us. He didn't even need it. He did it just to spite us."

Emma took a deep breath, trying to piece together the puzzle. The Rossi-Castello feud had been going on for generations, growing more bitter with each passing year. It wasn't hard to imagine how the tensions could have escalated to the point where someone might have wanted Victor out of the way—for good.

"But you didn't take revenge for that, did you?" Emma asked, her tone even but probing.

Luca's eyes flashed with anger, but he held her gaze. "I told you, Detective—I don't need to get my hands dirty. Victor got what was coming to him in the end. I didn't have to lift a finger."

The bitterness in his voice was unmistakable, and while Luca's words didn't directly incriminate him, they left Emma with an uneasy feeling. He might not have acted on his anger, but that didn't mean someone else in his orbit hadn't. The Rossi-Castello feud was more than just old business—it was personal, deeply personal, and the kind of hatred that had been cultivated for generations didn't just disappear.

As the sun finally dipped below the horizon, casting the vineyard in shadow, Emma realized that she was only scratching the surface of what was really going on here. The rivalry between the Rossi and Castello families wasn't just a backdrop to Victor's death—it was central to it.

The bitter harvest of years of resentment and grudges had finally come to bear. And now, it was up to Emma to find out just who had decided that it was time for the feud to end—with blood.

Part 2: Roots of Betrayal
Chapter 7: The Will

The mood in the Castello estate was thick with tension as the family gathered in the grand sitting room, waiting for the lawyer to arrive and reveal the contents of Victor's will. The large windows, which usually allowed the bright afternoon light to flood the room, felt oppressive today. Heavy drapes blocked out the autumn sun, casting the space in dim light. The silence was only broken by the faint ticking of the antique clock that hung on the wall—a reminder that time was passing, and soon, the future of the Castello legacy would be laid bare.

Emma Cross stood quietly near the doorway, observing. She had been invited to witness the reading, and though the lawyer had assured her it was a mere formality, she knew better. Wills often stirred up emotions and tensions long buried. In families as powerful and complex as the Castellos, they could do more than just divide property; they could break already fragile relationships.

Seated across from her, the Castello family members sat in varying degrees of composure. Isabela, Victor's widow, was perched on the edge of her chair, her back straight and her face set in an unreadable mask. The years of living with Victor had left their mark on her, Emma imagined. But today, there was no sign of grief—only a cold, steely resolve.

Next to her sat Marco, his fingers drumming impatiently on the armrest of his chair. He had always assumed he would inherit the lion's share of the vineyard, having been the one most involved in its day-to-day operations. But as the oldest son, Marco seemed to feel more entitled than the rest. His posture was tense, as though preparing for battle.

Alessandro, the younger son, sat slouched in his chair, his body language a stark contrast to his older brother's. He looked uncomfortable, almost detached, as though the whole thing didn't concern him. But Emma noticed the way his eyes flicked from Marco to their mother, and then toward the closed door. He may have acted indifferent, but something about the will clearly weighed on his mind.

And finally, Adriana. She sat elegantly, one leg crossed over the other, her lips curled in a faint, almost amused smile. Unlike her brothers, Adriana had never cared for the vineyard—or so she had claimed. Her interests had always lain elsewhere, but Emma had learned to be wary of those who appeared indifferent. She watched Adriana carefully, noting the glint in her eyes that suggested she might be anticipating more than anyone else realized.

The door creaked open, and the family lawyer, an older man named Carlo Esposito, entered the room, carrying a thick envelope. His expression was serious, but then again, it always was. Carlo had served the family for decades and had navigated countless disputes between them. But today, even he seemed a little more sombre than usual.

"Good afternoon," Carlo said, clearing his throat as he approached the large wooden desk in the center of the room. He glanced briefly at Emma, acknowledging her presence, before turning to face the family. "I'm here to read the last will and testament of Victor Castello."

The room seemed to hold its breath as Carlo unfolded the document. Emma could feel the tension rising, each family member bracing for what was to come.

"As you know," Carlo began, "Victor was a meticulous man, and he made several updates to his will over the years. This final version was executed just six months ago."

Six months ago. Emma's ears perked up at that. What had changed in Victor's life at that time to prompt such a recent update to his will? The land deal with the Rossis? Or perhaps something more personal?

Carlo continued. "The bulk of the estate, including Castello Vineyards, has been left to Marco Castello, as expected. Marco, you will inherit full ownership of the vineyard and all business-related assets, as well as the estate itself."

Emma watched Marco as he sat up straighter, his fingers stilling on the armrest. He gave a single, firm nod, his face betraying no surprise. This was what he had always believed would happen—it was his birthright, after all.

But then Carlo cleared his throat again, shifting slightly. "However, there are some additional provisions."

Marco's eyes narrowed, and Emma saw his jaw tighten.

"Victor has stipulated that 20% of the vineyard's annual profits will be allocated to Alessandro Castello," Carlo said, glancing at the younger brother. "This is in recognition of his contributions to the financial side of the business."

Alessandro blinked, seemingly caught off guard. He sat up a little straighter, his slouched posture disappearing as he absorbed the information. A look of surprise flashed across his face, quickly followed by one of relief. Perhaps he had expected nothing, and this, while not ownership, was more than he'd hoped for.

But it wasn't the end.

"Adriana Castello," Carlo said, turning his attention to the daughter who had remained so aloof. "Your father has left you a controlling share—30%—of the family's external investments, including the wine distribution company and various partnerships."

Adriana's smile widened ever so slightly. She uncrossed her legs, leaning forward as though the conversation had just gotten interesting. She nodded gracefully, as though it had all been part of her plan.

Emma noticed Marco shift in his seat. He had expected Adriana to be left out of the vineyard entirely, but this—while separate from the land—still gave her significant power over the family's financial interests.

"And finally," Carlo said, his voice softening, "Victor left a personal letter to Isabela Castello, his wife."

Carlo paused, his eyes meeting Isabela's for a moment before continuing. "While Isabela is not involved in the direct inheritance of the vineyard or business assets, Victor left her the contents of a personal account—a sum meant to ensure her comfort for the rest of her life."

Emma noticed a flicker of something in Isabela's eyes—disappointment? Or was it anger? The lack of direct control over the vineyard had surely stung, even though she had never been publicly involved in its management. But Emma had a feeling that Isabela had expected more—much more.

As Carlo folded the will and placed it back in the envelope, the room seemed to sink into silence, each member of the Castello family processing what had just happened.

But the calm didn't last long.

"This is ridiculous," Marco spat suddenly, his face flushed with anger. He stood abruptly, glaring at Carlo, then turning his fury toward his siblings. "I should have full control. I'm the one who's been running the vineyard! Why does Alessandro get any part of this? He's barely lifted a finger for the business!"

Alessandro bristled, standing to face his brother. "I've handled the finances, Marco! You think the vineyard runs on grapes alone? You would have run this place into the ground if I hadn't been managing the books."

"And Adriana?" Marco continued, ignoring Alessandro as he shot a furious look at his sister. "She doesn't even care about the vineyard, and now she gets to control our investments?"

Adriana raised an eyebrow, her voice icy. "Don't be so dramatic, Marco. I never wanted the vineyard, but I'm more than capable of handling the business side of things. Father trusted me with this. You, on the other hand, should be grateful for what you've been given."

The argument grew heated quickly, with Marco shouting accusations, Alessandro firing back with his own retorts, and Adriana fanning the flames with cutting remarks. Emma stood by, watching the family unravel before her eyes.

Isabela remained seated, her hands still clasped in her lap, but Emma saw the tightness in her jaw, the way her eyes had hardened into something cold and calculating. She wasn't saying anything, but it was clear that she had been expecting something different from Victor's will. Perhaps she had hoped for more influence, more control. Instead, she had been left with a token inheritance while her children warred over the future of the family's legacy.

Emma stepped forward, her voice cutting through the escalating argument. "I understand that this is a difficult moment for all of you, but there's something important to keep in mind. Victor updated his will only six months ago. I need to know—was there anything significant happening around that time? Any changes in the family dynamic?"

The question hung in the air, silencing the room for a moment.

Marco looked toward the floor, his face still red with anger. Alessandro stared out the window, and Adriana's lips curled into a knowing smile, though she said nothing.

Isabela's voice broke the silence, calm but icy. "Victor was not an easy man to live with, Detective. And in his last months, he became even more difficult. I suspect he made changes to his will based on whatever whims came to him in the moment."

Emma nodded slowly, though she suspected there was more to it than just whims. Victor's decisions about the inheritance seemed carefully calculated—designed not just to divide his assets but to stoke the fires of rivalry between his children.

The reading of the will had done more than simply divide Victor Castello's legacy. It had exposed the raw nerves of a family already fractured by ambition, resentment, and betrayal. And as Emma stood among the brewing storm, she couldn't shake the feeling that this was only the beginning of a much deeper, darker conflict.

A conflict that might have been the true cause of Victor's death.

Chapter 8: Wine and Poison

The air in the vineyard was cool and still as Detective Emma Cross stood near the spot where Victor Castello's body had been found. The vines swayed gently in the breeze, as though whispering secrets to each other, while the sun dipped low on the horizon, casting long shadows over the rows of grapes. What had once been a peaceful setting now felt ominous. The more she investigated, the clearer it became that Victor's death wasn't just an unfortunate accident. The question now was whether someone had a hand in it.

Emma had been piecing together the family dynamics, but something else had been gnawing at her ever since the forensic team had mentioned the strange markings found on both Victor's body and the vines. Those marks—the discoloration, the burns—had stayed in her mind, echoing alongside a growing suspicion.

Chemicals.

The vineyard was no stranger to pesticides and other agricultural treatments, of course. But the damage she'd seen didn't seem like the usual kind. And then there was the blood in the soil, the crushed grapes mixed with something darker. Could Victor's death be connected to something toxic—something more deliberate?

She turned as the sound of footsteps approached. Gina, the forensic specialist, walked over, carrying a file in her hand.

"Detective, we've got some preliminary results back from the lab," Gina said, her expression serious. "There's something you'll want to see."

Emma took the file, opening it as she began to walk toward the vineyard's storage shed. The pages revealed the lab's findings, and immediately, a few key details stood out: traces of certain chemicals had been found in both Victor's bloodstream and in the soil where his body had been discovered. But these weren't just normal vineyard pesticides. Some of them were far more potent—and dangerous.

"What am I looking at here?" Emma asked, her eyes narrowing as she scanned the results.

"We found small amounts of copper sulphate and another chemical compound—this one's harder to identify, but it's not something typically used in vineyards," Gina explained. "Copper sulphate is common in vineyards for pest control, but in high concentrations, it can be toxic. The other substance, though, is more concerning. It's something that could be lethal in small doses. Our toxicology team is still trying to determine exactly what it is."

Emma's mind raced as she processed the information. Copper sulphate could explain the markings on Victor's skin and the vines, but the presence of an unidentified chemical—something stronger—added a new layer to the investigation. If it wasn't a standard pesticide, then someone could have introduced it deliberately. Poison.

"Do we know how this other substance could have been administered?" Emma asked, already thinking through the possibilities.

"We're still looking into that," Gina said. "It could have been ingested, or it might have been absorbed through the skin. There were no clear signs of ingestion, like stomach contents pointing directly to poison, but the chemical burns on Victor's skin suggest that he came into contact with it somehow—either through touch or exposure."

Emma closed the file and exhaled slowly, her suspicions hardening into something more concrete. Victor's death wasn't a natural one. He had been poisoned—whether intentionally or accidentally remained to be seen, but the presence of such dangerous chemicals couldn't be a coincidence. Someone had access to these substances, and someone had a motive.

"Let's check the vineyard's storage for any of these chemicals," Emma said, leading Gina toward the storage shed at the far end of the property. "I want to know if this was something easily accessible or if someone went out of their way to get it."

The shed was an old, sturdy structure with a heavy wooden door. Emma pulled it open, revealing shelves stocked with various bottles and containers, each labelled with the names of pesticides, fertilizers, and other vineyard essentials. The scent of chemicals hung in the air, sharp and pungent.

Gina joined her, scanning the labels. "Copper sulphate, potassium bicarbonate... these are all standard for treating vines. Nothing unusual so far."

Emma crouched down to inspect the lower shelves, her eyes searching for anything out of place. Most of the containers looked like they had been sitting there for years, their labels faded and their caps covered in dust. But then something caught her eye—tucked behind a row of older bottles was a small, unlabelled vial. It was clean, new, and out of place among the other containers.

Emma reached for it carefully, holding it up to the light. The liquid inside was clear, but something about the vial felt wrong. Why was it hidden? And why didn't it have a label?

"What do you think?" Emma asked, showing the vial to Gina.

Gina's eyes widened slightly. "That's definitely not standard. We'll need to take it back to the lab for analysis, but if I had to guess, it could be some kind of industrial-strength pesticide—or worse."

Emma's gut churned. Someone had hidden this here for a reason. It wasn't the sort of thing you just forgot about. The question was: who had access to the vineyard's storage, and who would have had a reason to introduce such a dangerous chemical?

As she stood there, holding the vial, Emma's mind returned to the Castello family. She thought of the will, the tensions that had exploded when Victor's final wishes were revealed. There were more than enough motives to go around. Marco, with his simmering resentment over his father's control of the vineyard. Alessandro, desperate for a greater role in the business. Adriana, calculating and detached, but far from innocent. And Isabela, who had lived with Victor's domineering presence for years, quietly nursing her own grievances.

But would any of them go so far as to poison him?

Emma's thoughts were interrupted by the sound of a voice calling her name. She turned to see Marco approaching, his expression unreadable.

"What are you doing in here?" Marco asked, his voice edged with suspicion.

"I'm just following up on some leads," Emma replied evenly, tucking the vial into her evidence bag. "We've found traces of chemicals near where your father was found. I'm trying to determine if they were connected to his death."

Marco's eyes narrowed. "Chemicals? You think he was poisoned?"

Emma didn't answer directly. "Do you know if anyone else has access to this storage area?"

Marco folded his arms, his gaze hard. "The workers do, but it's mostly me. I manage the day-to-day operations. No one comes in here without my permission."

Emma held his gaze, searching for any hint of deception. "Have there been any incidents lately? Anything unusual in the vineyard—sabotage, accidents?"

Marco hesitated, his jaw tightening. "We've had issues before. People trying to mess with our equipment, workers not following protocol. But nothing serious. At least, nothing I thought was serious."

Emma filed that away, watching him closely. "When was the last time you checked the chemicals in the shed?"

"I don't know," Marco said, shifting uncomfortably. "A few weeks ago, maybe. I've been busy with the harvest."

Emma's mind churned. Marco had the most to gain from his father's death—he was the primary heir to the vineyard, after all. But was that enough to drive him to murder? And if it wasn't Marco, then who had the opportunity and the knowledge to pull off such a deliberate act?

As she prepared to leave the shed, Emma's phone buzzed. A message from the lab: Preliminary results on the unidentified chemical suggest a highly toxic compound used in industrial farming—banned in most countries due to its lethal effects on humans.

Emma's heart raced as she read the words. Someone had poisoned Victor Castello, and they had used a substance so dangerous that it had been outlawed in most places. This wasn't just an accident. It was intentional.

She slipped the phone back into her pocket, her mind racing as she walked past Marco, who was watching her closely.

"We'll be in touch," Emma said, her voice steady, though her thoughts were anything but.

As she left the vineyard, the shadows growing long in the fading light, she knew one thing for certain: someone in the Castello family—or someone close to them—had access to deadly chemicals and the motive to use them.

Now, it was a matter of finding out who had turned the vineyard from a place of harvest into a place of death.

Chapter 9: Secrets in the Cellar

The cool, damp air of the Castello wine cellar clung to Detective Emma Cross as she descended the narrow stone steps, her flashlight slicing through the darkness. The cellar was vast, a labyrinth of shelves and barrels filled with the finest vintages Castello Vineyards had produced over the years. The earthy smell of aging wine mixed with the faint scent of mildew, creating an atmosphere both rich and foreboding.

Emma had spent most of the day piecing together new clues from the investigation. Victor Castello's poisoning had raised more questions than answers, and while the vineyard's storage shed had offered some insight, she had a growing suspicion that the vineyard's secrets ran much deeper than just dangerous chemicals. Her conversation with Marco earlier had been unsettling, and she couldn't shake the feeling that the answers she needed were hidden somewhere on the estate.

The wine cellar had always been off-limits to anyone outside the family. According to the workers, Victor had kept the cellar locked at all times, allowing only a select few access to its contents. Marco had the key now, but Victor's control over this space had been absolute while he was alive. Emma wondered what he had been keeping down here—beyond the prized vintages and the history of the Castello family's wine business.

She ran her hand along the cold stone walls, feeling the chill seep through her fingers. The cellar was well-organized, with rows of neatly labelled wine bottles, each categorized by year and variety. But Emma wasn't here for the bottles on display. She was searching for something hidden.

Earlier that day, while speaking with one of the vineyard's long-time employees, a cryptic comment had caught Emma's attention. The worker, an old man named Pietro, had mentioned "a room beneath the cellar" but quickly clammed up when pressed for details. It was clear he hadn't meant to say anything at all, but the words had been enough to spark Emma's curiosity. If there was a secret room in the cellar, what had Victor been hiding?

Emma moved deeper into the cellar, her footsteps echoing softly on the stone floor. The further she went, the darker it became, the air thicker with moisture. She kept an eye out for any signs of something out of place—loose stones, concealed doors, anything that might indicate a hidden space.

Her flashlight beam flickered across an old wine barrel tucked into a shadowy corner, its wooden surface weathered and worn. Something about the barrel caught her attention. Unlike the others, it wasn't labelled, and it seemed heavier, more solid, as though it hadn't been moved in years. She knelt down and ran her fingers along its edge, feeling for a latch or seam. Sure enough, after a few moments of searching, her hand brushed against a hidden lever disguised as part of the barrel's wooden frame.

With a soft click, the barrel shifted slightly, revealing a narrow stone door behind it. Emma's pulse quickened as she pushed the door open, the heavy stone groaning as it swung inward. Beyond the door was a small, dimly lit room, no larger than a closet, hidden away from the rest of the cellar.

Emma stepped inside, her flashlight casting long shadows across the walls. The room was lined with shelves, but instead of the neatly organized bottles she had seen in the main cellar, these shelves were filled with a different kind of wine. The bottles here were expensive—rare vintages from some of the most exclusive vineyards in the world. Some were clearly collectors' items, their labels faded and their glass dusted with age. Others were new, pristine, and clearly worth a fortune.

But it wasn't the wine that drew Emma's attention. It was what else the room held.

On the far wall, stacked behind the bottles, were several ledgers and boxes of documents. Emma pulled one of the ledgers off the shelf and flipped it open. The entries were written in Victor's neat, methodical handwriting, but as she scanned the pages, her eyes widened. These weren't just business records. They were details of transactions—sales, shipments, and payments made under the table.

Several of the entries referenced specific dates and shipments of wine, but the destinations listed were suspicious. Countries with strict import restrictions, places where Castello Vineyards shouldn't have been legally exporting. The amounts involved were staggering, and Emma quickly realized that this was no ordinary business dealing. Victor had been using his vineyard to facilitate illegal wine sales—likely smuggling high-end bottles into black-market channels to avoid taxes and regulations.

Emma set the ledger aside and pulled out another, her heart racing. This one was worse. Not only did it list more illegal transactions, but it also named several people who appeared to be connected to the deals—high-profile buyers, distributors, and even a few names that sent a chill down Emma's spine. Some of the transactions were tied to notorious black-market wine traders known for moving illicit goods across borders. If Victor had been dealing with them, he had been playing a very dangerous game.

She set the second ledger down and moved toward one of the boxes, opening it carefully. Inside, she found a stash of sealed wine bottles, each labelled with a number rather than a name. She frowned, examining one closely. The label was a counterfeit, meant to look like an exclusive Castello vintage, but something was off. The production dates didn't match the vineyard's official records. Was Victor selling counterfeit wine along with the legitimate shipments? It seemed likely.

Emma stood back, staring at the shelves in shock. Victor had been running an underground operation, using his vineyard's reputation to mask a much darker side of the business. The question now was whether his death had anything to do with it. Had one of his illegal dealings gone wrong? Had someone discovered the secret and decided to silence him?

Her thoughts were interrupted by the sound of footsteps echoing down the cellar steps. Emma tensed, quickly shutting the door to the hidden room and covering the entrance with the barrel again. She moved back toward the main section of the cellar just as Marco appeared at the bottom of the stairs, his face hard.

"What are you doing down here?" Marco asked, his voice sharp, his eyes narrowing with suspicion.

"I'm following up on some leads," Emma replied calmly, though her heart was still racing from what she had just discovered. She needed to play this carefully. "I thought it would be a good idea to check the cellar. Sometimes records get stored down here that don't make it to the office."

Marco's gaze flickered toward the corner where Emma had been moments before, but he didn't press the issue. "You're wasting your time," he said dismissively. "There's nothing down here but wine."

"Maybe," Emma said, watching him carefully. "But I've learned that people often hide things in plain sight."

Marco smirked, but it didn't reach his eyes. "If you say so, Detective. But I think you're looking in the wrong place. My father's secrets weren't in his wine. They were in his head."

Emma kept her expression neutral, though Marco's words only confirmed her suspicions. Victor Castello had been hiding something big, and now that Emma had uncovered his secret stash, the pieces of the puzzle were starting to fall into place. The illegal deals, the counterfeit wine, the connections to dangerous people—it all pointed to a life lived in the shadows, even while Victor had maintained his public image as a respected winemaker.

As Marco turned to leave, Emma's mind churned with possibilities. Victor's death could have been the result of any number of things—family resentment, business rivalries, or perhaps even a deal gone wrong. The illegal wine trade could have made him enemies, people who wouldn't hesitate to eliminate him if he became a liability.

But there was one thing Emma was certain of now: Victor's death wasn't just about family or inheritance. It was about power, greed, and the secrets he had kept hidden in the dark corners of his vineyard. And whoever had killed him had known exactly what they were doing.

As she turned back toward the cellar's exit, Emma felt a cold certainty settle over her. She had uncovered part of Victor Castello's dark legacy. Now, she had to find out who had wanted him dead—and what price they had been willing to pay to protect their own secrets.

Chapter 10: The Last Vintage

The air was thick with anticipation as Detective Emma Cross sat in Victor Castello's private tasting room, a place reserved only for the vineyard's most exclusive guests. It was a luxurious space, its walls lined with carefully curated bottles of wine from Castello Vineyards' most successful years. The rich mahogany table in front of her gleamed under the warm light of the chandelier, casting soft shadows across the room. The scent of aging oak and the faint trace of grapes lingered in the air, giving the space an aura of refined tradition.

Yet today, the room felt different—heavy, laden with tension.

Emma had been hearing whispers about Victor's last project since the beginning of the investigation. An exclusive, limited-edition vintage that Victor had been meticulously crafting, something that was supposed to elevate the Castello name even higher in the world of fine wines. This wasn't just any wine; it was rumoured to be extraordinary, a product of years of perfecting blends and experimenting with techniques handed down through generations. Victor's crowning achievement. And now it had become a central piece of the puzzle she was trying to solve.

As Emma waited for Marco to join her, she thought about what this vintage represented. For a man like Victor, obsessed with legacy, this wine wasn't just a business venture—it was the culmination of everything he had worked for. Could it have been worth killing for?

The door creaked open, and Marco entered the room, his expression serious. He had been more cooperative since their tense encounter in the cellar, though Emma could sense a growing frustration in him. He was a man under pressure, balancing the weight of his father's legacy, his own ambitions, and now, the shadow of a murder investigation hanging over his family's vineyard.

"You wanted to know about the last vintage," Marco said, walking over to the large wooden cabinet that stood against the far wall. His voice was steady, but there was a hint of weariness in it. "Well, here it is."

He unlocked the cabinet and pulled out a bottle, holding it up to the light. The bottle was elegant, with a sleek black label embossed with the Castello family crest. The year—this year—stood out in gold, marking it as the final creation of Victor Castello. It was beautiful, almost too perfect, like an artifact from another time. Emma couldn't help but feel a strange reverence as she gazed at it.

"This was supposed to be the game-changer," Marco said, setting the bottle down carefully in front of Emma. "My father called it his masterpiece. He had been working on it for years, blending different grapes, experimenting with aging techniques. He said it would be the wine that defined our family for generations."

Emma looked up at Marco, studying his face. There was pride there, but also something else—something darker. "And what do you think?" she asked. "Was it really that important to him?"

Marco hesitated, then sat down across from her. "It was everything to him. He was obsessed with it. More than with the vineyard itself, more than with us." He sighed, running a hand through his hair. "To him, this wasn't just a wine. It was his legacy. He was so sure that it would win every award, get international acclaim, and cement our name forever. He wanted to leave behind something untouchable."

Emma nodded slowly, letting the words sink in. "Was anyone else involved in the production of this vintage? Any outside experts, consultants?"

Marco shook his head. "No. My father didn't trust anyone with this. He kept the process secret. Only a few of us even knew about it—me, Alessandro, and a couple of the winemakers. He was paranoid about it getting out, afraid someone would try to steal the formula."

Emma's mind whirred. The secrecy surrounding the vintage was striking. If Victor had been so protective of it, then it wasn't just a business venture. It was a closely guarded secret, one that could have been worth a fortune on the open market. But it also meant that only a small group of people had access to the process—and, potentially, a motive for murder.

"Was the wine ready for release?" Emma asked, her eyes narrowing as she leaned forward. "Was there any particular event or deadline approaching that would have put pressure on your father?"

Marco hesitated again, and Emma saw the tension in his jaw as he answered. "Yes. He had planned to unveil it at a private event—an exclusive tasting for a group of critics and buyers. It was set for next week."

The timing struck Emma immediately. Victor's death had come just before the big reveal. Whoever had killed him had likely known about the tasting, about the importance of this vintage. Had they wanted to stop the event—or perhaps take control of it?

"Who was invited to this tasting?" Emma asked, her voice firm.

Marco shrugged, though the movement seemed forced. "The usual suspects—top wine critics, some wealthy buyers, potential investors. My father was hoping to attract more international partners. He wanted this vintage to be the one that broke us into new markets, beyond Europe."

Emma's thoughts raced. The tasting could have been the perfect opportunity for someone to sabotage Victor's plans, to take his masterpiece and claim it for themselves. But it also opened up a new set of suspects—people from outside the family, buyers and critics who might have had their own reasons for wanting to get their hands on the wine.

"You said only a few people knew about the production," Emma said, her eyes narrowing as she considered the implications. "But did anyone try to interfere? Did your father ever mention feeling threatened?"

Marco's face darkened. "He didn't talk about it much, but I know he was paranoid. He thought someone was trying to sabotage the vineyard—messing with the barrels, contaminating the vines. A few times, we found signs that someone had tampered with the wine storage, but nothing serious ever came of it. My father dismissed it as carelessness from the workers."

"Could it have been something more?" Emma pressed. "Could someone have been trying to sabotage this vintage?"

Marco exhaled sharply, shaking his head. "I don't know. It's possible. My father had plenty of enemies in the business. Other winemakers, distributors, even some of the critics who didn't like him. He wasn't exactly well-loved."

Emma thought back to the rivalry with Luca Rossi and the underhanded tactics that had been mentioned during her investigation. If someone had wanted to sabotage the Castello family's final masterpiece, it could have been a powerful blow to Victor's legacy—and a powerful motive for murder.

But there was another possibility, one that Emma couldn't ignore.

"Marco," Emma said, her voice low and steady, "was there anyone in the family—anyone close to your father—who stood to gain from controlling this vintage? Anyone who might have seen this wine as their opportunity?"

Marco's expression shifted, and for the first time, Emma saw real hesitation in his eyes. He glanced down at the bottle, his fingers tapping nervously on the table. "You mean... Alessandro or Adriana?"

Emma didn't say anything, letting the question hang in the air.

Marco leaned back in his chair, his face tense. "Alessandro's always been more interested in the financial side of things. He doesn't care about the wine itself, but he knows how valuable this vintage is. As for Adriana... well, she never cared about the vineyard, but she's smart. She knows how much influence this wine could bring. I wouldn't put anything past her."

Emma took a deep breath, sensing the widening cracks in the family's unity. The stakes were higher than ever now. Victor's last vintage wasn't just wine—it was power, money, and legacy, all wrapped up in one bottle. And someone had wanted it enough to kill for it.

As she stood to leave, Marco's eyes followed her, the tension still thick in the air.

"Detective," he said quietly, his voice barely more than a whisper, "if you find out that one of us did this... what happens to the vineyard?"

Emma didn't answer immediately. Instead, she picked up the bottle of the last vintage, turning it in her hands before setting it back down on the table.

"The truth always has consequences," she said softly, meeting his gaze. "And this vineyard may never be the same again."

As Emma walked out of the tasting room, the weight of the investigation pressing down on her, she knew one thing for certain: Victor's masterpiece had been worth killing for. Now it was up to her to figure out who had decided that his last vintage would also be his last breath.

Chapter 11: The Widow's Grief

Detective Emma Cross had never been one to trust appearances, and as she sat across from Isabela Castello in the grand sitting room of the Castello estate, that scepticism was working overtime. Isabela, ever poised and composed, looked every bit the grieving widow. Dressed in a black dress that clung modestly to her frame, her dark hair pulled back in a loose bun, and her eyes faintly red, she embodied the image of a woman mourning the loss of her husband. Yet, despite the outward display of grief, something about Isabela's behaviour set off alarm bells in Emma's mind.

It wasn't just her calmness—some people grieved differently, after all. It was the small details, the subtle cracks that had begun to form in her story, little contradictions that Emma couldn't ignore.

"I still can't believe he's gone," Isabela said softly, her hands resting in her lap, fingers twisting a delicate silver bracelet around her wrist. Her voice was low, almost too controlled. "Victor was always such a strong presence in this house. His absence is... overwhelming."

Emma nodded, watching Isabela closely. She had come to speak with her again, not just to offer condolences, but to probe deeper into her alibi. Isabela had claimed she'd been at the house the night of Victor's death, reading in her private sitting room. She said she hadn't seen or heard anything until Marco found the body early the next morning.

But Emma had learned that grief had a way of exposing the truth, and the more time that passed, the more things started to seem... off.

"I'm sure it's been difficult," Emma said, her tone measured. "Losing a husband so suddenly—especially someone as important to the family as Victor."

Isabela's lips tightened into a small, thin smile. "He was everything to this family. A powerful man. He built all of this with his bare hands. It's hard to imagine life without him."

That much was true. Victor's personality had been larger than life, and his control over the vineyard—and the family—had been absolute. But Emma suspected that beneath the surface of Isabela's quiet grief lay something else. She couldn't ignore the growing list of inconsistencies that had begun to surface about the night Victor died.

"Isabela," Emma said, leaning forward slightly, her voice soft but probing, "there's something I'd like to clarify with you. You mentioned earlier that you were in the house all evening when Victor was at the vineyard. But I spoke with a few of the household staff, and one of them mentioned seeing you leaving the estate around nine that night. Could you explain that?"

Isabela's eyes flickered for a brief moment, her composure faltering ever so slightly. "I... I went for a drive," she admitted, her voice steady but quieter now. "I needed some air. The stress of everything—it's been difficult."

Emma raised an eyebrow. "You didn't mention that before."

"I didn't think it was important," Isabela said quickly, her tone sharpening just a fraction. "I was only gone for a short time. I needed to clear my head."

Emma nodded, but the excuse felt too convenient. Isabela had clearly withheld that detail on purpose, and now that it had been brought to light, her defensiveness suggested there was more she wasn't saying.

"Where did you go?" Emma asked, her voice calm but insistent.

Isabela hesitated for just a moment too long. "I drove down to the village. I didn't stop anywhere, I just... needed to be alone."

Emma let the silence hang in the air between them for a few moments before responding. "The staff mentioned seeing your car returning around midnight. That's a long time to drive around the village, don't you think?"

Isabela's eyes darkened, and for the first time, Emma saw something flicker behind her calm exterior—irritation, perhaps even anger. "Are you suggesting I had something to do with Victor's death, Detective?"

Emma leaned back slightly, keeping her expression neutral. "I'm just trying to understand the timeline, Isabela. We're still piecing together what happened that night, and your movements are important."

For a long moment, Isabela said nothing. Her fingers continued to twist the bracelet on her wrist, her knuckles white with tension. Finally, she spoke, her voice low and controlled.

"Victor and I had our... differences," she said slowly. "Our marriage was not perfect. I'm sure you've heard that from others by now."

Emma nodded. The tension between Victor and his wife had been well known, at least to those within the family. Isabela had been a constant presence by his side, but rumours of his cold, domineering behaviour—and perhaps his infidelities—had swirled for years. It wasn't hard to imagine that their marriage had been one of convenience rather than love in its final years.

"Differences?" Emma prompted.

Isabela looked up at Emma, her dark eyes hardening. "Victor was a difficult man. He was controlling, obsessive. He wanted everything to be his way, and he expected everyone to fall in line. Including me." She paused, her voice growing bitter. "But I had my own life before him. My own identity. And over the years, I felt that slipping away."

There it was. Emma could hear the resentment in Isabela's words, the pent-up frustration of a woman who had been pushed to the margins of her own life, living under the shadow of a husband who never let her forget who was in control.

"Did you ever think about leaving?" Emma asked, watching Isabela carefully.

Isabela laughed softly, a bitter sound that echoed through the room. "Leave? No, Detective. I'm not a fool. This estate, this vineyard—everything I've worked for, everything I've built alongside Victor—it would have been taken from me. I would have been left with nothing."

Emma nodded slowly. That made sense. Isabela had been tied to Victor through the vineyard, through their shared wealth and status. Leaving would have meant losing everything. But staying… that had its own price.

"Did Victor know how you felt?" Emma asked quietly.

Isabela's jaw tightened. "Victor knew everything. He always knew. But he didn't care. He was focused on the vineyard, on his legacy, on his precious last vintage. I was just… there."

Emma's eyes sharpened at the mention of the vintage. "Was the vineyard more important to him than the family?"

Isabela didn't answer immediately. She stood from her seat and walked toward the window, staring out at the vast rows of vines that stretched across the property. For a long moment, she was silent.

"When Victor started working on that last vintage, he became obsessed," Isabela said, her voice distant. "It was all he talked about, all he thought about. He shut everyone out—even me. He was convinced it would be the wine that made him a legend."

Emma stood and moved to stand beside Isabela, watching the vineyard with her. "But you didn't share his obsession."

Isabela shook her head, her face unreadable. "No. I didn't care about the wine. But I cared about what it meant. Victor was going to leave everything to Marco, to the vineyard. The will he drew up made that clear. I would be left with little more than the house—and none of the power."

Emma felt a chill run down her spine. There it was again: the will. Isabela had known that she would be left with little control over the vineyard, over the empire she had helped build. Had that been enough to push her over the edge?

"Is that why you were out that night?" Emma asked softly. "Did something happen between you and Victor?"

Isabela turned to face Emma, her expression hardening once more. "I didn't kill my husband, Detective. I may have hated what he became, but I would never have killed him. I may have lost my place in this family, but I am not a murderer."

Emma studied her for a long moment, weighing the truth of her words. Isabela was a master at hiding her emotions, but the contradictions in her story—the late-night drive, her bitterness toward Victor—suggested that she knew more than she was letting on.

"Then why lie about your whereabouts that night?" Emma asked quietly.

Isabela's gaze turned cold. "Because I know how this looks. I know what you're trying to suggest. But I won't be your scapegoat, Detective."

With that, Isabela turned and walked toward the door, her posture stiff and unyielding. Emma watched her leave, the tension in the room thick enough to cut through. The widow was grieving, yes, but Emma couldn't shake the feeling that Isabela's grief was hiding something far more dangerous.

As Emma stood alone in the grand sitting room, she considered everything Isabela had said—and everything she hadn't. The contradictions in her story were too glaring to ignore, and while Isabela may not have pulled the trigger—or poured the poison—Emma had a strong feeling she was more involved than she wanted to admit.

And now, Emma had to find out just how far Isabela had been willing to go to protect her place in the Castello legacy.

Chapter 12: Tangled Vines

Detective Emma Cross stood at the edge of the vineyard, watching the workers move methodically through the rows of vines. The rhythmic sound of shears clipping grape clusters filled the air, accompanied by the low murmur of conversation among the labourers. The sun was high overhead, casting a golden light over the land, but beneath the peaceful surface, Emma could sense tension simmering.

The Castello vineyard had always been a source of pride for the family, but it was also a battleground. Not just between the family members themselves, but between the workers who toiled in the fields. Rumours had been swirling for years about ongoing disputes between the Castello workers and those from the neighbouring Rossi vineyard. These weren't just typical rivalries between vineyards—they were deeply rooted in family feuds, stretching back generations.

Emma had come to the vineyard today to dig into those tensions. She'd heard whispers from some of the staff about arguments, sabotage, and old grudges between the Castello and Rossi workers. If these disputes had escalated, they could provide a key piece of the puzzle in Victor's death.

She made her way down the rows of vines until she reached a small group of workers taking a break near the equipment shed. They glanced up at her approach, their faces cautious, but not unfriendly. One of them, an older man with weathered skin and deep-set eyes, stood up and nodded in greeting.

"Detective," the man said, his voice rough from years of work outdoors. "You're here about the boss, aren't you?"

Emma nodded. "I need to ask you all some questions. I've heard that there have been tensions between the workers here and those over at the Rossi vineyard. Can you tell me more about that?"

The man—Pietro, she recalled—exchanged a glance with the others before turning back to her. "Tensions is putting it lightly. There's been bad blood between the Castellos and the Rossis for as long as I can remember. And it's not just the families. The workers feel it, too."

Emma's eyes narrowed. "What kind of bad blood?"

Pietro sighed and wiped the sweat from his brow. "The Rossis have always tried to push us around. They think their vineyard's better, that they make better wine, and that we're all just riding on their coattails. It started with the bosses, sure—Victor and Luca never could stand each other—but it's been passed down to the workers. Fights, sabotage, insults... it's like a never-ending war."

Emma leaned against the shed, arms crossed. "Sabotage? Can you give me some examples?"

One of the younger workers, a wiry man named Franco, chimed in. "We've had tools go missing, irrigation lines cut, even a few grape shipments spoiled because someone got into our storage. It's always little things—nothing we can ever prove came from the Rossi side, but we all know. It's been going on for years."

"And has it ever escalated beyond that?" Emma asked, her voice calm but probing.

Pietro hesitated, exchanging another glance with Franco and the others. "There've been fights, here and there. Mostly when we're out in the village. You know how it is—after a few drinks, things get heated. We've had some scuffles with the Rossi men. But it's never come to anything serious."

Emma frowned. "And recently? Has anything changed between the two vineyards?"

Pietro's expression darkened. "Ever since Victor started working on that new vintage, things have gotten worse. The Rossis knew about it—everyone in the valley did. Victor was putting everything into it, and it made Luca Rossi furious. He thought Victor was trying to overshadow them, to make the Castello name the biggest in the region. That stirred up the old rivalry all over again."

Emma nodded. She had already heard about the Rossi family's resentment over Victor's ambitious plans for the vineyard's last vintage, but hearing it from the workers gave her a new perspective. The rivalry wasn't just about business or family pride—it was about control, about dominance in the region's wine industry. And that rivalry had trickled down to the workers, who were caught in the middle of the feud.

"Did Victor ever mention any specific threats from the Rossis?" Emma asked, her eyes on Pietro. "Did he think they would try to sabotage the vintage?"

Pietro shifted uncomfortably, glancing at the other workers before speaking. "Victor didn't trust Luca, that's for sure. He thought the Rossis would try something—maybe mess with the vines or the barrels. But he didn't seem to think it would go beyond that. Not... not to the point of killing someone."

Emma's mind raced as she considered Pietro's words. The Rossis had a clear motive to sabotage Victor's last vintage, but could their anger have escalated to murder? If Victor had been poisoned, as the evidence suggested, it was possible that someone on the Rossi side had wanted to stop him from releasing the wine. But how far would they have gone?

"And what about the workers?" Emma asked, her tone sharper now. "Could any of the Rossi workers have been involved in something more serious—something that could have led to Victor's death?"

Franco stepped forward, his face grim. "There's one guy—Paolo. He's been working for the Rossis for years, and he's got a reputation for causing trouble. He's always stirring things up, always looking for a fight. If anyone from the Rossi side would've crossed a line, it'd be him."

Emma's interest piqued. "Paolo? Has he ever had any direct confrontations with Victor or the Castello workers?"

Pietro nodded. "A few months ago, Paolo and some of his men got into it with us at a bar in the village. They were drunk, talking about how the Rossi vineyard would crush Castello's last vintage, how Victor was just an old man clinging to a dying legacy. Things got heated, and Paolo threatened Marco. Said the Castello name wouldn't mean anything when they were done."

Emma's pulse quickened. "Did Victor know about this?"

Pietro shook his head. "Marco didn't tell him. He didn't want to worry his father."

Emma made a mental note to follow up on Paolo. If the tension between the workers had escalated to the point of open threats, it was possible that someone from the Rossi side had seen Victor's death as a way to end the feud once and for all.

But there was another layer to this, one that Emma couldn't ignore. The rivalry between the families and their workers wasn't just about business—it was about pride, about legacy, and about control. And if someone had felt threatened enough by Victor's success, by his plans for the future, they might have been willing to go to extreme lengths to protect their own.

"Thank you for your time," Emma said, nodding to the group. "If you think of anything else—anything at all—please let me know."

As she turned to leave, Pietro's voice stopped her. "Detective... do you think the Rossis had something to do with Victor's death?"

Emma paused, glancing back at him. "I don't know yet. But I'm going to find out."

Pietro's eyes darkened, and he shook his head. "Be careful. This feud... it runs deep. Deeper than most people realize."

Emma nodded, understanding the weight of his words. The rivalry between the Castello and Rossi families wasn't just a matter of business competition—it was a tangled web of history, pride, and resentment. And as Emma left the vineyard, she couldn't shake the feeling that unravelling that web would reveal far more than she had bargained for.

As she walked back toward the estate, her mind churned with the possibilities. The long-standing feud between the workers, the threats, the sabotage—all of it pointed to a conflict that had been building for years. But had it finally boiled over into murder?

Emma knew she was getting closer to the truth, but the more she uncovered, the more dangerous the path ahead became. The vines at Castello Vineyard were tangled with secrets, and soon, those secrets would come to light—no matter the cost.

Part 3: Barrels of Lies
Chapter 13: Unfiltered Truth

Detective Emma Cross had seen it before: secrets festering beneath the surface of a family, hidden so deeply that they were almost invisible until something—usually a tragedy—brought them bubbling up. And in the Castello family, secrets were as plentiful as the grapes on their vineyard. Today, as she pieced together yet another fragment of the puzzle surrounding Victor Castello's death, Emma had a sinking feeling that she was about to uncover something that could turn the entire investigation on its head.

Sitting at the small café in the nearby village, Emma sipped her coffee and reviewed her notes. The feud between the Castello and Rossi families had already proved more dangerous than she'd anticipated, with tensions simmering not just between the vineyard owners, but also among the workers. The rivalry between the two vineyards had been passed down through generations, and the stakes had never been higher, especially with Victor's last vintage on the line. But something else was nagging at Emma's mind—an inkling that there was more to Marco's involvement in the family business than just loyalty to his father.

She had received a tip earlier that morning, an anonymous message left on her phone with a cryptic warning: Marco isn't the loyal son he pretends to be. Check his connections with the Rossi vineyard. The message had been vague, but it was enough to send Emma digging. A quick inquiry around the village had led her to a name she hadn't expected: Sofia Romano, one of the Rossi vineyard workers. Rumours had swirled around Sofia for years—she was known for her beauty and sharp wit, but also for stirring trouble. And now, it seemed, her name was linked to something far more dangerous: Marco Castello.

Emma had arranged to meet Sofia in the back of a small, dimly lit tavern on the edge of the village, far from the prying eyes of the vineyard workers. When Sofia arrived, she was dressed casually, her long dark hair tied back in a loose ponytail. Her eyes were guarded, but Emma could tell she was nervous—her hands fidgeted slightly as she sat down across from the detective.

"You're Sofia Romano?" Emma asked, her tone gentle but firm.

Sofia nodded, her gaze darting around the room. "I don't know why you wanted to talk to me, Detective," she said cautiously. "I don't know anything about Victor's death."

Emma leaned in slightly, lowering her voice. "I think you know more than you're letting on. You worked at the Rossi vineyard, but I've heard rumours that you had a… connection to Marco Castello."

Sofia's eyes widened slightly, but she quickly composed herself. "I don't know what you're talking about."

Emma gave her a level look. "I think you do. You and Marco were involved, weren't you? A secret relationship between the Castello heir and a worker from the Rossi vineyard. It's the kind of scandal that could've destroyed both families if it got out."

Sofia tensed, her lips pressing into a thin line. For a moment, it seemed like she might deny everything, but then her shoulders sagged, and she let out a long sigh.

"We were careful," she said softly, her voice barely above a whisper. "But I guess nothing stays hidden forever."

Emma's heart quickened. She had been right—Marco had been keeping a dangerous secret. "How long?" she asked. "How long were you and Marco seeing each other?"

Sofia glanced down at the table, her fingers tracing the edge of her glass. "A few months. It started as… I don't even know. It wasn't supposed to be serious. But Marco—he's not like the rest of them. He hates the feud. He wanted to get away from all of it."

Emma frowned. "But he didn't. He stayed. Why?"

Sofia's eyes darkened. "Because of his father. Victor had this... hold on him. He couldn't escape, no matter how much he wanted to. He kept telling me he was going to leave, that we'd go somewhere far away and start over. But I knew it was just a fantasy."

Emma could see the pain in Sofia's expression, the way she was torn between anger and sadness. "Did anyone else know about the two of you?"

Sofia hesitated, then nodded. "Luca Rossi found out a few weeks ago. He saw us together—he was furious. He warned me to stay away from Marco, but I couldn't. I was... in too deep."

Emma's mind raced. Luca Rossi had known about the affair. If Victor had found out, it would have been a scandal that could have destroyed the Castello family's reputation. Could that have been the motive? Had someone killed Victor to prevent the truth from coming out?

"Did Marco ever talk about his father's plans?" Emma asked, her tone sharpening. "About the vineyard, the last vintage?"

Sofia's gaze flickered with something Emma couldn't quite place—fear, maybe? Or guilt? "He didn't tell me much," Sofia said slowly. "But I know he was under a lot of pressure. His father was obsessed with the vintage, and Marco... Marco didn't care about the vineyard as much as Victor wanted him to. He was torn between wanting to make his father proud and wanting to be free of him."

Emma leaned forward. "Sofia, I need you to be honest with me. Did Marco ever talk about doing something to stop his father? Anything that might suggest he was desperate enough to..."

Sofia's eyes widened in alarm. "No, Detective! Marco wouldn't hurt his father. He hated him sometimes, sure, but he never would have—" She stopped, shaking her head. "He wouldn't have killed him."

Emma wasn't so sure. Marco had been hiding a lot, and if he had been desperate enough, if he had seen no other way out, perhaps he had been driven to take drastic measures. But whether it was Marco or someone else in the family, the affair had added a new layer to the investigation.

"Where is Marco now?" Emma asked, her voice tight.

"I don't know," Sofia said softly. "We haven't spoken since Victor died. I think he's scared. I think he's afraid the truth is going to come out."

Emma stood, her mind already racing ahead to what she needed to do next. If Marco was hiding, it was because he knew that his secrets were starting to unravel. And if Sofia was right—if Luca Rossi had known about the affair—it added a whole new dimension to the Rossi-Castello feud.

As Emma left the tavern, the weight of the unfiltered truth settled heavily on her shoulders. The affair between Marco and Sofia was more than just a scandal—it was a potential motive, a reason for someone to act out of fear, desperation, or revenge.

Emma's next move was clear: she needed to find Marco before the truth caught up to him. And as she walked through the village, the sun casting long shadows over the narrow streets, she couldn't help but wonder if Victor Castello's death was the result of more than just a family feud. It was becoming increasingly clear that the tangled web of lies, secrets, and betrayals stretched far beyond the vineyard itself.

And now, with Marco's hidden affair exposed, it was only a matter of time before the entire Castello empire came crashing down.

Chapter 14: The Vineyard Heir

Detective Emma Cross stood in the grand foyer of the Castello estate, her mind a swirl of conflicting theories. The deeper she delved into Victor Castello's death, the more tangled the motives became. The affair between Marco and Sofia Romano had been a revelation, exposing not only Marco's discontent but the intensity of the longstanding feud between the Castello and Rossi families. But now, her attention was shifting to someone else—someone who had been lurking in the shadows of the investigation: Adriana Castello.

Adriana had always been a mystery, even to those who knew her best. Sharp, ambitious, and often overlooked by her father, she had managed to distance herself from the family vineyard, focusing on other interests, cultivating a life beyond the grapes and vines. But Emma had come to realize that distancing herself from the family business didn't mean Adriana didn't care about it. In fact, she had begun to suspect that Adriana cared deeply—perhaps enough to kill.

The more Emma dug, the more she found cracks in the carefully constructed facade Adriana presented to the world. For years, Victor had favoured Marco as the heir to the Castello vineyard, passing over Adriana despite her business acumen and sharp intelligence. And now, in the wake of Victor's death, it was becoming increasingly clear that Adriana had wanted control of the vineyard—and she had never forgiven her father for denying her that chance.

Emma's suspicions had been growing ever since she'd spoken with Marco earlier in the investigation. Despite his own frustrations with his father, Marco had hinted that Adriana had always resented being sidelined. And with Victor's sudden death, it seemed possible that Adriana had finally seen an opportunity to claim what she believed was rightfully hers.

Emma was about to confront her.

Adriana was in the drawing room when Emma entered. The room, like the rest of the estate, was opulent, with large windows overlooking the sprawling vineyard and ornate furniture that spoke to generations of wealth. Adriana sat on a velvet armchair, a glass of red wine in hand, looking every bit the poised, composed woman she was known to be. She glanced up as Emma approached, her expression calm but her eyes sharp.

"Detective," Adriana greeted her coolly. "I take it you're here to ask more questions."

Emma gave her a polite nod. "I am. I'd like to talk to you about your role in the family business, Adriana."

Adriana raised an eyebrow, swirling the wine in her glass. "I think you already know that I was never truly involved in the vineyard. My father made sure of that."

Emma took a seat across from her, watching her carefully. "That's precisely why I wanted to speak with you. You weren't involved, but not because you didn't want to be. From what I've learned, you were interested in taking over the vineyard, but Victor didn't see you as the heir."

Adriana's lips curled into a faint smile, though there was no warmth behind it. "You've done your homework, Detective. Yes, I was interested in the vineyard at one point. I had ideas for expanding the business, taking it in a new direction. But my father was a traditionalist. He didn't think I had the right 'touch' for winemaking."

Emma leaned forward slightly, her tone measured. "That must have been frustrating. Especially since you have a strong business background. From what I understand, you would have been a capable leader for the vineyard."

Adriana's eyes flashed briefly, a hint of something darker passing through her expression. "Frustrating doesn't begin to cover it," she said, her voice tight. "Marco was always his favourite when it came to the vineyard. My father thought winemaking was a man's world, something

Marco could carry on while I was left to... what? Organize charity events and play the dutiful daughter? He never took me seriously, and that was his mistake."

Emma's heart quickened as she sensed the shift in Adriana's tone. Beneath her calm exterior, there was a well of resentment that had been building for years. Adriana had wanted control, and she had been denied—repeatedly.

"You must have felt betrayed," Emma said softly. "After all, you've proven yourself in other areas of business. And now, with your father's death, the vineyard could finally be within your grasp."

Adriana's eyes narrowed, and for a moment, the mask slipped. Her jaw tightened, and she set her wine glass down with deliberate care.

"What are you implying, Detective?" Adriana asked, her voice cold.

Emma met her gaze evenly. "I'm saying that Victor's death benefits you, Adriana. With him gone, there's a chance you could take over the vineyard—something you've wanted for a long time."

Adriana stood abruptly, her posture rigid as she moved to the window. She stared out at the vineyard, her back to Emma, and for a moment, neither of them spoke. The silence stretched on, heavy and charged.

Finally, Adriana spoke, her voice quiet but laced with bitterness. "I won't deny that I resented my father's decisions. He underestimated me, kept me at arm's length, even when I could have helped him build something greater. But do you really think I'd kill him for it?"

Emma stood as well, keeping her voice calm but direct. "I think you had a lot to gain from his death. The vineyard is a powerful asset, and you've shown that you have the ambition to take control of it. You've been passed over for years—was that enough to push you to act?"

Adriana turned to face her, and for the first time since Emma had arrived, there was real emotion in her eyes. Anger, frustration, and perhaps even a hint of sorrow.

"You have no idea what it was like to live under my father's rule," Adriana said, her voice trembling with barely suppressed rage. "He controlled everything—every decision, every aspect of our lives. I worked my entire life to prove myself, to show him that I was capable. And what did I get for it? Nothing. I was always the 'other child,' the one he dismissed."

Emma took a step closer. "That sounds like a powerful motive, Adriana. You've been fighting for control your whole life."

Adriana's expression hardened. "You think I wanted this? That I wanted to take over the vineyard by force? No, Detective. You're wrong. Yes, I wanted to prove myself to my father, but not like this. If I had wanted to take over, I would have done it on my terms—not through some backhanded plot."

Emma studied her, searching for any signs of deception. Adriana was passionate, angry even, but was it enough to kill?

"You have to admit, the timing is convenient," Emma said quietly. "Victor was about to release his last vintage, and with him gone, the vineyard's future is uncertain. It gives you an opening."

Adriana's gaze sharpened. "I didn't kill my father, Detective. I'm not a monster. But don't think for a second that I won't fight for what's mine now that he's gone."

Emma didn't flinch at Adriana's fierce tone. If nothing else, she believed Adriana when she said she would fight. The question was, had she already started that fight before Victor's death?

As Emma turned to leave the room, Adriana's voice stopped her.

"You're looking in the wrong place," Adriana said, her voice cold and measured once more. "Marco has always been the one with something to prove. Maybe you should be asking him what he was willing to do to hold onto the vineyard."

Emma paused, glancing back at Adriana. She was a skilled manipulator, but there was something in her words that gave Emma pause. Marco had been favoured by Victor, but that didn't mean he hadn't had his own reasons for wanting control. And now, with both siblings pointing fingers at one another, Emma knew that the truth was buried somewhere between their accusations.

As Emma left the estate and walked through the vineyard, she couldn't shake the feeling that Adriana was hiding more than she let on. She had ambition, drive, and resentment—all dangerous ingredients in a family already teetering on the edge of collapse. But was it enough to push her to murder?

With each step, Emma felt the vines of the Castello legacy tightening around her investigation. And as she moved closer to the truth, she realized that the heir to the vineyard might not be the only one with secrets to protect.

Someone had killed Victor Castello. Now, it was just a matter of uncovering who.

Chapter 15: Corked Evidence

Detective Emma Cross had walked the halls of the Castello estate more times than she cared to count since the investigation began. But today felt different. The air was charged with a sense of urgency as she made her way toward Victor Castello's private office. Something had been nagging at her—something subtle but persistent. The missing piece she had been searching for, the one that might finally connect the dots and bring the truth of Victor's murder into the light.

Victor's office was a place of power, tucked away in the far corner of the sprawling villa. Unlike the rest of the estate, which was all grandeur and opulence, the office was surprisingly modest, designed with function in mind. Heavy wooden shelves lined the walls, filled with ledgers, documents, and years of business records for the vineyard. It was clear that this was where Victor had run his empire—meticulously, relentlessly, and alone.

Emma had combed through the office before, looking for anything out of place, any detail that might offer insight into Victor's final days. But this time, she had a specific goal in mind. After her conversation with Adriana, Emma was more convinced than ever that the key to solving the case lay in Victor's relationship with the vineyard, particularly his obsession with the last vintage. And if Victor had been hiding something in his office, she was determined to find it.

The room was dimly lit, with the late afternoon sun casting long shadows through the narrow windows. Emma moved to the large oak desk in the center of the room, her eyes scanning the surface. It was neat, almost too neat. A stack of invoices sat to one side, a pen perfectly placed beside a leather-bound notebook. But it was the cabinet behind the desk that drew Emma's attention. The first time she'd inspected the office, she'd barely glanced at it—assuming it was nothing more than storage for business records and wine contracts. Now, she felt a pull toward it, an instinct telling her that something important was hidden inside.

Emma walked over to the cabinet and opened it, revealing rows of carefully arranged files and a few bottles of wine. Most of the bottles were labelled with the Castello vineyard's signature crest, but one bottle, tucked into the farthest corner, stood out.

It was different—unlabelled, with a darker glass, and covered in a thin layer of dust. Unlike the other bottles, which had been displayed openly, this one seemed intentionally hidden.

Emma's pulse quickened as she reached for the bottle, her fingers brushing against the cold glass. There was something off about it. It felt heavier than a normal wine bottle, and as she held it up to the light, she noticed a faint residue around the cork. The cork itself was worn, slightly discoloured, as if it had been tampered with.

Her mind raced. Could this be it? Could this be the link she'd been searching for?

Emma set the bottle on the desk and pulled on a pair of gloves from her bag. She carefully removed the cork, the familiar sound of its release echoing softly in the quiet room. The scent that emerged was unmistakable—wine, yes, but something else. Something sharp, chemical, and wrong. Her stomach turned as she realized what she was smelling.

Poison.

Emma's heart pounded in her chest as she stared at the bottle, her mind flashing back to the initial findings from the toxicology report. The presence of chemicals on Victor's body, the strange burns on the vines—could this bottle be the missing piece? Had Victor been poisoned with wine?

She looked more closely at the residue on the cork. It was faint, but unmistakable—a thin, almost oily substance that had soaked into the cork and stained the lip of the bottle. Someone had tampered with this wine, and it hadn't been done accidentally.

Emma carefully re-corked the bottle, her mind racing with possibilities. If Victor had drunk from this bottle, it would explain the presence of chemicals in his system. But why had it been hidden in his office? Was he planning to drink it himself, or had someone planted it there, knowing he would eventually open it?

Her thoughts were interrupted by the sound of footsteps outside the office door. Emma tensed, quickly placing the bottle back in the cabinet and closing it. The door creaked open, and Marco stepped inside, his face a mixture of surprise and suspicion.

"Detective Cross," he said slowly, his eyes narrowing as he glanced around the room. "What are you doing in my father's office?"

Emma turned to face him, keeping her expression neutral. "Just following up on some leads. I was going through Victor's records again, trying to piece together the events leading up to his death."

Marco's gaze lingered on the cabinet behind her, but he didn't push the issue. "Have you found anything?" he asked, his voice tense.

Emma studied him for a moment, considering her next move. She wasn't ready to reveal what she had found just yet—not until she had more information. But Marco's sudden appearance made her wonder. Was he hiding something? Did he know about the poisoned bottle?

"Nothing concrete," Emma said smoothly, walking around the desk to face him more directly. "But I did want to ask you about the wine. Your father's last vintage was a major project for him, wasn't it?"

Marco nodded, though his jaw tightened slightly. "Yes. It was his obsession. He believed it would be the pinnacle of our family's legacy."

"And did your father have any bottles that were... off-limits? Special bottles he didn't want anyone to touch?" Emma asked, her tone casual but watchful.

Marco hesitated, and for the briefest moment, his eyes flicked toward the cabinet where Emma had found the suspicious bottle. "He was particular about his wine, yes. He had certain bottles he kept for himself—rare vintages, ones that were important to him."

"Important enough that he'd keep them hidden?" Emma pressed.

Marco's face hardened, and he took a step closer to her. "What are you getting at, Detective? My father's wine was everything to him. But if you're suggesting that one of those bottles had something to do with his death..."

Emma held his gaze, unflinching. "I'm suggesting that your father's death wasn't an accident. And that there are things about his final days—about the vineyard—that don't add up. I need to know if anyone else had access to his private collection of wine."

Marco's expression darkened, and for a moment, Emma saw the flicker of something behind his eyes—fear, perhaps, or guilt. He opened his mouth to respond, but before he could speak, the door to the office swung open again, and Alessandro stepped in.

"Detective," Alessandro said, his tone clipped, his eyes darting between Emma and his brother. "What's going on?"

Emma took a step back, her attention now divided between the two brothers. The tension between them was palpable, and as they stood there, staring at each other, Emma couldn't help but wonder how deep the rivalry between them truly went.

"I'm just following up on a few things," Emma said, her voice calm. "I'll be in touch soon."

Without waiting for a response, Emma slipped past the two brothers and left the office, her mind buzzing with the implications of what she had found.

The bottle of poisoned wine was the key. She was sure of it. But now she had to figure out who had planted it, and why. Was it Marco, desperate to secure his place as the rightful heir to the vineyard? Or had someone else—perhaps Alessandro, or even Adriana—decided that Victor's obsession with the vineyard had become too dangerous?

As Emma walked out into the crisp air of the vineyard, she knew one thing for certain: the Castello family's secrets were slowly unravelling, and the corked evidence she had found in Victor's office was just the beginning.

The vineyard had become a battleground, and someone was willing to kill to keep control of it.

Chapter 16: The Vintner's Apprentice

The crisp autumn air carried the familiar scent of fermenting grapes as Detective Emma Cross made her way through the vineyard toward a small cottage nestled on the edge of the estate. The contrast between the beauty of the rolling hills and the darkness she'd uncovered in the Castello family was striking. The vineyard, with its endless rows of grapevines stretching toward the horizon, seemed so peaceful, yet underneath it all lay a tangled web of secrets, greed, and now, murder.

Today, Emma was meeting with someone she hoped could shed new light on the investigation: Matteo, a young winemaker who had worked under Victor Castello for several years. He had left the estate abruptly a few months before Victor's death, and Emma had recently learned that his departure wasn't as amicable as it had been made to seem. Whispers around the vineyard suggested that Matteo had seen too much—perhaps too much for Victor's liking.

When Emma arrived at the small cottage, she found Matteo waiting outside, leaning against the doorframe. He was in his late twenties, with dark hair that curled slightly at the ends and a youthful intensity in his eyes. His clothes were casual, but Emma noticed the slight tension in his posture, the way he crossed his arms defensively as she approached.

"Detective Cross," Matteo greeted her, his voice cautious but polite. "I wasn't expecting to hear from you."

Emma smiled, though her expression remained serious. "I appreciate you agreeing to meet with me, Matteo. I understand you used to work closely with Victor Castello."

Matteo's face darkened slightly at the mention of Victor's name, and he uncrossed his arms, gesturing for Emma to follow him inside. The interior of the cottage was simple but cozy, with wooden beams overhead and the smell of freshly baked bread lingering in the air. Emma could see that Matteo had carved out a quiet life for himself after leaving the vineyard, but the shadow of his time there seemed to hang over him.

Once they were seated, Emma got straight to the point. "I know you left the Castello vineyard a few months ago. What I'm interested in is why. From what I've gathered, it wasn't just a matter of moving on to other opportunities."

Matteo shifted uncomfortably, running a hand through his hair. "No, it wasn't," he admitted, his voice quiet. "Victor and I... we didn't exactly see eye to eye in the end."

Emma leaned forward, her tone gentle but probing. "Can you tell me why? From what I've heard, you were one of his most promising winemakers. He trusted you with a lot."

Matteo let out a bitter laugh. "Trusted me? Maybe at first. But that changed when I started asking questions."

Emma raised an eyebrow. "Questions about what?"

Matteo hesitated, glancing toward the window as if checking to see if anyone could hear them. After a moment, he sighed and turned back to Emma. "Victor wasn't the man everyone thought he was. Sure, he was a brilliant winemaker, but he wasn't ethical. Not by a long shot."

Emma's heart quickened. This was what she'd been hoping for. "What do you mean by unethical?"

Matteo's expression grew serious. "Victor had a lot of dirty business practices. For one, he cut corners where he could. He used chemicals on the vines that were banned in most places—strong pesticides and fertilizers that could boost the yield but were dangerous. He didn't care about the health risks, not to the workers or the land."

Emma's mind flashed back to the toxicology report and the strange markings on Victor's body and the vines. "Are you saying he used these chemicals even though he knew they were harmful?"

Matteo nodded. "Yes. He was obsessed with perfection. He didn't care how it was achieved, as long as the wine looked and tasted perfect. And those banned chemicals—he sourced them from shady suppliers, people who operated outside of the law. I tried to bring it up, tried to warn him that it was dangerous, but he shut me down every time."

Emma's stomach churned. This revelation fit with the growing picture of Victor as a man driven by ambition and willing to cross any line to secure his legacy. But it also raised new questions about the circumstances of his death. Had someone finally retaliated against Victor for his unethical practices?

"Did anyone else know about this?" Emma asked. "Were there others who confronted Victor?"

Matteo leaned back in his chair, his gaze distant as if remembering those tense final days at the vineyard. "A few of the workers knew. We saw things—chemicals being stored where they shouldn't be, shipments coming in at odd hours. But no one had the courage to speak up. Victor had a way of keeping people in line, and those who challenged him... well, they didn't last long at the vineyard."

Emma thought of the other workers she had interviewed. None had mentioned anything about these illegal practices, but then again, fear could keep people silent.

"And what about his family?" Emma asked, her voice steady. "Did they know?"

Matteo's eyes flickered with something unreadable. "Marco and Alessandro knew something, I'm sure of it. Marco had more involvement in the vineyard, but I think even he tried to stay in the dark about the worst of it. He didn't want to cross his father. As for Adriana..." Matteo hesitated, then shook his head. "She wasn't involved with the vineyard directly, but she knew Victor was up to something. I could tell."

Emma frowned. This was exactly the kind of information she had been hoping to find—evidence that Victor's actions had alienated not just his workers, but perhaps even his family. It also reinforced her growing suspicion that Victor's death wasn't just about the inheritance or family rivalries. It could be tied to these dangerous business practices—practices that had put many lives at risk.

"Did Victor ever express concern that his actions might catch up with him?" Emma asked, her mind racing.

Matteo's face grew grim. "Not exactly. But a few weeks before I left, there was an incident—someone sabotaged one of the shipments. It was a batch of chemicals that Victor was expecting, but when it arrived, it had been tampered with. He was furious. He thought someone was trying to ruin him."

Emma's pulse quickened. "Do you know who might have been behind it?"

Matteo shook his head. "No. But I remember him saying that if anyone ever tried to take the vineyard from him, they'd regret it."

Emma's thoughts whirled as she processed Matteo's words. The sabotage, the chemicals, the growing tension around Victor's unethical practices—this was all starting to fit together. Someone had known about Victor's dangerous actions, and they had wanted to stop him. But who? Was it a worker? A family member? Or one of the shady suppliers Victor had dealt with?

"What about Victor's last vintage?" Emma asked. "Did you have any involvement in that?"

Matteo's expression darkened further. "I helped with it in the early stages, but by the time I left, Victor had taken over completely. He didn't want anyone else touching it. That vintage... it was his obsession. He believed it would make him untouchable."

Emma nodded slowly, understanding the weight of what Matteo was saying. Victor had been a man consumed by ambition, willing to cut corners, break the law, and put others at risk to achieve his vision. But that vision had ultimately led to his death.

Emma stood, thanking Matteo for his time. As she left the cottage, the crisp air hit her, clearing her mind. The pieces of the puzzle were finally starting to come together. Victor's unethical business practices had created enemies—both within and outside of the vineyard.

And now, someone had taken matters into their own hands. Someone who had known about the chemicals, about the danger Victor had put the vineyard and its people in.

As Emma walked through the vineyard, the sun setting behind the hills, she knew one thing for certain: the vines held more than just the secrets of winemaking. They held the truth of Victor's death, and Emma was getting closer to uncovering it.

The vineyard's dark history was about to be exposed, and whoever had corked the bottle of poisoned wine had done so to protect far more than just a legacy.

Chapter 17: Grapes of Wrath

The tension inside the Castello estate had become as thick and oppressive as the late summer heat that blanketed the vineyard. Detective Emma Cross stood near the doorway of the main sitting room, watching as Marco and Alessandro Castello circled each other like lions preparing for a fight. Their tempers had been simmering for days, but now, in the wake of the revelations about their father's unethical business practices, the fragile peace between the brothers was about to shatter.

"You've always been the golden boy, Marco, but you're nothing without Father!" Alessandro's voice echoed through the grand room, his frustration spilling over. His face was flushed, his posture rigid with anger. "You think you're the heir to the vineyard, but all you've done is mismanage everything."

Marco, taller and broader than his younger brother, stood near the fireplace, his arms crossed over his chest. His jaw was clenched, his eyes hard with barely controlled fury. "Don't talk to me about mismanagement, Alessandro. You were never around. You only cared about the vineyard when it suited your interests—when there was money to be made."

Alessandro took a step closer, his fists balled at his sides. "You've been running this place into the ground. Father trusted you, and you've let it fall apart. The vineyard was supposed to be our legacy, but thanks to you, it's on the verge of collapse. How many deals have you botched, Marco? How many times have you made decisions that put us in jeopardy?"

Emma could feel the weight of their words, the deep-rooted resentment that had been brewing between the brothers for years. She had always sensed the tension between them, but now it was erupting, and with every accusation they hurled at each other, she could see how Victor's death had exacerbated their simmering rivalry.

"You think I wanted this?" Marco spat, his voice rising. "You think I asked to be the one handling all of Father's mess? Do you know how much pressure I've been under? Father wasn't the saint you're making him out to be, Alessandro. He cut corners, made shady deals, and pushed everyone to the brink. I'm the one who had to clean up after him!"

Alessandro scoffed, his face twisting with bitterness. "Don't pretend like you were the hero, Marco. You went along with everything Father did. You knew about the chemicals, the illegal shipments—you're just as guilty as he was!"

At that, Marco's expression darkened further. He took a threatening step toward Alessandro, his voice low and dangerous. "Careful what you're accusing me of, little brother. You were never part of this business because you never cared enough to be. You were too busy chasing your own ambitions."

Emma knew she had to step in before the confrontation escalated further. She took a deep breath and stepped forward, her voice cutting through the tension. "Enough! Both of you."

The brothers turned to her, their anger still radiating from them like heat, but they held back, clearly aware of her presence as an investigator. Emma could feel the raw emotion in the room—this wasn't just a fight about business; it was about power, control, and years of unresolved jealousy.

"I've heard enough blame being thrown around," Emma said firmly. "But let's focus on what's important here: your father's death. The vineyard may be in turmoil, but Victor's death was no accident. And both of you need to start working together if we're going to find out what really happened."

Marco scoffed, but his voice was quieter now, more measured. "Working together? With him? How can I trust someone who's been out for himself this whole time?"

Alessandro glared at Marco but said nothing, his silence speaking volumes. The divide between them was deep, and it was clear that years of rivalry had left scars that neither brother was willing to address.

Emma turned to Alessandro, her voice steady. "Alessandro, you've accused Marco of mismanaging the business. But you've been away from the vineyard for most of its operations. Do you know about the chemicals your father was using? About the shortcuts he was taking?"

Alessandro shifted uncomfortably, avoiding Marco's gaze. "I... I knew something was wrong, but I didn't know the details. I didn't want to be involved in the day-to-day running of the vineyard. Father always made it clear that it was Marco's responsibility."

"But you still benefited from the vineyard's success, didn't you?" Emma pressed. "Even if you weren't directly involved, you knew the vineyard's financial health was tied to your own future."

Alessandro's face flushed with embarrassment, and he crossed his arms defensively. "I wasn't profiting off Father's dirty deals, if that's what you're implying. I had my own business ventures."

Marco scoffed again, this time with a bitter laugh. "Your own business ventures? You're just like Father—obsessed with the bottom line. The only difference is you didn't have to get your hands dirty."

Alessandro's eyes narrowed, and he took a step closer to Marco. "And you did? Is that what you're saying, Marco? That you had no choice but to be part of his schemes?"

Emma watched the exchange closely, her mind racing. The more the brothers argued, the more it became clear that Victor had kept secrets from both of them—secrets that had shaped the vineyard's operations in ways they were only now beginning to understand. But Marco had been closer to those secrets, more involved in the vineyard's shady dealings, while Alessandro had kept himself at arm's length. The question was: who stood to gain the most from Victor's death, and had either of them been desperate enough to kill for it?

"Marco," Emma said, turning to him, "you were your father's right hand in the vineyard. You've been managing the business since he started planning the last vintage. Did you ever feel like you were losing control of the vineyard? That your father's decisions were putting you—and the family—at risk?"

Marco's face tightened, and for a moment, Emma thought he might refuse to answer. But then he exhaled, his shoulders sagging slightly. "I hated what Father was doing. I hated the risks he was taking, the corners he was cutting. But he was relentless. He wouldn't listen to me, wouldn't even consider that there might be a better way to run the vineyard. I tried to keep everything together, but it was like... like trying to control a storm."

Emma nodded, sensing the frustration in his voice. "So you felt trapped. Like you had no choice but to follow his lead."

Marco's eyes met hers, and for the first time, she saw something vulnerable beneath his hardened exterior. "Yes. I was doing everything I could to keep the vineyard afloat, but every decision he made pushed us closer to the edge. I didn't want to lose everything we had built."

Emma turned to Alessandro. "And you, Alessandro? You weren't involved in the vineyard's operations, but you still had a stake in its success. How did you feel about your father's choices?"

Alessandro's jaw clenched, and his voice was tight when he spoke. "I hated what he was doing, too. But unlike Marco, I didn't let myself get sucked into it. I stayed away because I knew it was all going to fall apart eventually."

The tension in the room was palpable, and Emma could feel the weight of their words. Both brothers had been trapped by their father's decisions—Marco by his involvement in the vineyard, and Alessandro by his distance from it. But now, with Victor dead, the vineyard's future was in their hands, and the blame they had been throwing at each other was tearing them apart.

"You both need to understand something," Emma said, her voice firm. "Your father's death wasn't just the result of his bad business practices. Someone took advantage of the chaos in this family, and you're both playing into it by blaming each other. If you want to save the vineyard, if you want to find out who killed your father, you need to stop fighting and start working together."

The brothers stared at each other for a long moment, the anger between them still simmering but tempered by Emma's words. Finally, Marco spoke, his voice quieter now. "You're right, Detective. We've been too busy tearing each other apart to see what's really going on."

Alessandro nodded, though the tension between them remained. "This vineyard is our legacy. We can't let it die with Father."

Emma watched them carefully, knowing that their cooperation was fragile at best. The Castello brothers had been at odds for years, and it would take more than a single conversation to bridge the divide between them. But for now, they had a common goal: finding out the truth about Victor's death.

As she left the estate, Emma knew the investigation was entering its most dangerous phase. The brothers might have agreed to work together, but the vineyard's tangled history—and the secrets it held—were far from being fully revealed.

And somewhere, amidst the vines and the legacy, the truth about Victor's murder was waiting to be uncovered.

Part 4: Barrel Aging
Chapter 18: The Harvest Celebration

The Castello vineyard's annual Harvest Celebration was a time-honoured tradition, a grand event that brought together the local community, vineyard workers, and the powerful families of the wine industry. It was a moment to celebrate the bounty of the harvest, the culmination of months of hard work, and the promise of another fruitful year. But this year, the festival was different. The shadow of Victor Castello's death hung over the estate, casting a pall over the festivities that no amount of wine or laughter could fully dispel.

Detective Emma Cross walked through the large courtyard, her eyes scanning the crowd. Tables were set up with fine linens, and the air was filled with the scent of roasting meats and the rich aroma of wine. Lanterns hung from trees, casting a soft glow over the gathering as the sun dipped below the horizon. The vineyard was in full celebration mode, but there was an undercurrent of tension in the air—an unease that Emma couldn't ignore.

Emma had been invited to attend the festival, though her presence was less about celebrating and more about observation. The investigation into Victor's death had brought too many secrets to light, and Emma knew that with the entire Castello family gathered here, along with key figures from the community, this was an opportunity to watch the dynamics at play. With tempers still flaring between Marco and Alessandro and the unresolved mystery surrounding Victor's demise, the night promised to be revealing.

As Emma moved through the crowd, she noticed the strained smiles and whispered conversations. The vineyard workers were doing their best to enjoy the festivities, but the recent revelations about Victor's unethical practices had left many of them on edge. The

Castello family's reputation had taken a hit, and it seemed everyone was waiting for the next shoe to drop.

At the center of the courtyard, Marco and Alessandro stood at opposite ends of a long table, each surrounded by their own small group of guests. Their body language spoke volumes—Marco, tall and broad-shouldered, was doing his best to project an air of control, but there was a tightness in his jaw, a sign that the pressure of the last few weeks was weighing on him. Alessandro, on the other hand, looked restless, his eyes darting around the crowd, as though searching for an opportunity to make his move.

Emma could feel the tension between the brothers even from a distance. Despite their promise to work together to save the vineyard, their rivalry was still very much alive, simmering just below the surface. And tonight, at this public event, old wounds were bound to be exposed.

As Emma approached the table, she overheard a conversation between two vineyard workers.

"They say Victor wasn't the saint he pretended to be," one man whispered, his voice low. "Using banned chemicals, making shady deals... and now look what's happened. The vineyard's falling apart."

"Marco's no better," the other replied, shaking his head. "He's been running the place into the ground. Maybe Alessandro's the one who should be in charge."

Emma's ears perked up at the mention of Alessandro. The workers weren't the only ones questioning Marco's leadership; whispers had been circulating that Alessandro was quietly positioning himself to take control of the vineyard. With Victor gone, the power struggle between the brothers had only intensified.

As the evening progressed, the crowd gathered around the large outdoor stage, where speeches and toasts were about to begin. Marco stepped up to the microphone first, raising a glass of wine as he addressed the guests.

"Thank you all for being here tonight," Marco began, his voice steady but lacking its usual confidence. "This year's harvest has been difficult, but we're proud of what we've achieved. My father built this vineyard with his blood, sweat, and tears, and it's up to us to carry on his legacy."

Emma watched as Marco's gaze flicked toward Alessandro, the weight of his words hanging in the air. There was a subtle challenge in his tone, a reminder to his brother—and everyone else—that he was Victor's chosen heir.

Alessandro's jaw tightened, but he said nothing as Marco continued. "I know there have been rumours, questions about the future of the vineyard. But let me assure you, the Castello name is strong. We will endure, and we will continue to produce the finest wine this region has ever seen."

The crowd responded with polite applause, though Emma could sense the underlying doubt in their faces. The Castello name had been tarnished, and Marco's attempts to rally the crowd felt hollow.

As Marco stepped down from the stage, Alessandro pushed past him, grabbing the microphone before anyone else could speak. The crowd fell silent, sensing the brewing storm.

"My brother talks about legacy," Alessandro began, his voice sharp. "But legacy isn't just about tradition. It's about innovation, about moving forward. My father's way of doing things? It's outdated. And if we keep clinging to the past, this vineyard is doomed."

A murmur ran through the crowd, and Emma's heart raced. Alessandro wasn't just making a speech—he was challenging Marco's leadership in front of everyone.

"Father made mistakes," Alessandro continued, his eyes locking onto Marco's. "Mistakes that Marco has been covering up for years. The chemicals, the shady deals—it wasn't just Victor. Marco knew, and he did nothing. He let it happen."

The air seemed to thicken with the weight of Alessandro's accusations. Emma could see the shock on the faces of the guests, but it was Marco's reaction that caught her attention. His face had turned a deep shade of red, his fists clenched at his sides as he struggled to keep his composure.

"That's enough, Alessandro!" Marco barked, stepping forward. "You don't know what you're talking about."

"Oh, I know exactly what I'm talking about," Alessandro shot back, his voice rising. "You've been lying to everyone, pretending you're the perfect heir to the vineyard, but you're just as guilty as Father was. Maybe more."

The crowd was dead silent now, all eyes on the two brothers as their long-buried resentment boiled over in front of everyone.

"Do you really want to do this here?" Marco growled, his voice low and dangerous.

"Yes, Marco," Alessandro spat. "I do. Because it's time the truth came out. The vineyard deserves better. The people deserve better."

Marco lunged at Alessandro, grabbing him by the collar of his shirt, and for a moment, it seemed like the brothers might come to blows. Gasps rippled through the crowd as the tension reached its breaking point.

"Stop this!" Emma shouted, stepping forward to intervene.

Both brothers froze, their eyes locked in a deadly stare, the anger between them palpable. Emma could feel the weight of the family's history in that moment—the rivalry, the jealousy, the deep-seated wounds that had festered for years.

Emma stepped between them, her voice calm but firm. "This isn't the place for this. You're letting your father's legacy tear you apart, and that's exactly what someone wanted."

Marco released his grip on Alessandro, breathing heavily, while Alessandro stepped back, his eyes still blazing with anger.

The tension in the courtyard was suffocating, and Emma knew the damage had been done. The Castello brothers had publicly exposed their family's fractures, and there was no going back now. The vineyard's future was in jeopardy, and so was the family's fragile unity.

As the crowd slowly began to disperse, whispers of the brothers' fight rippling through the guests, Emma knew one thing for certain: the truth was closer than ever. The brothers' rivalry wasn't just about power—it was about survival. And in the heart of the vineyard, amidst the celebration that had turned into chaos, Emma sensed that Victor's death was tied to more than just business decisions.

Someone had wanted this fight to happen. Someone had known that exposing the cracks in the Castello family would bring everything crumbling down.

The real reckoning was yet to come.

Chapter 19: A Sour Note

The night air at the Castello vineyard's Harvest Celebration had grown colder, and so had the atmosphere. What had started as a tense family confrontation between Marco and Alessandro was now spiralling into something darker. Detective Emma Cross could feel the unease in the crowd as murmurs of the brothers' public clash spread, like wildfire catching hold of dry brush. But the evening was about to take another unexpected turn.

Emma had been watching the tension between the brothers unfold when she noticed a figure at the edge of the crowd—a man standing alone, his face obscured in the dim light of the lanterns. He was older, his posture hunched, but there was something about his presence that drew Emma's attention. His eyes were fixed on Marco and Alessandro, but they weren't filled with curiosity like the others. No, there was something else—bitterness, perhaps, or anger that had been simmering for years.

As the crowd began to thin out further, the man stepped forward, moving slowly but deliberately toward the stage where Marco and Alessandro still stood, their argument having subsided into a tense standoff. Emma's instincts flared, and she moved closer, sensing that whatever was about to happen could be important.

The man's voice cut through the murmur of the guests, loud and ragged, stopping everyone in their tracks.

"Is this what we're celebrating tonight?" he called out, his voice trembling with a mixture of fury and despair. "The Castello name? This vineyard? The lies?"

All eyes turned toward him, and a hush fell over the courtyard. Marco and Alessandro both looked toward the man, confusion and frustration flickering across their faces.

"Who are you?" Marco demanded, stepping forward. "What do you want?"

The man's eyes blazed with anger. "You don't remember me, do you, Marco? Or maybe you've tried to forget. My name is Enrico, and I worked for your father for over thirty years. I gave my life to this vineyard, just like so many others. And how did Victor repay us?"

Marco's face hardened. "This isn't the time for—"

"This is the time," Enrico interrupted, his voice rising. "It's time for the truth to come out. For years, Victor Castello built his empire on the backs of men like me, and he didn't care about the cost. Do you even know what happened to my family?"

Emma's heart pounded in her chest as she watched the scene unfold. Enrico's words were thick with emotion, and as he spoke, the weight of whatever he was about to reveal seemed to press down on the crowd.

Marco took a step closer, his eyes narrowing. "What are you talking about?"

Enrico's hands trembled as he pointed toward Marco. "I'm talking about the accident. The one Victor covered up. The one that killed my son."

A collective gasp rippled through the crowd, and Emma felt a chill run down her spine. Enrico's words hung in the air like a bitter echo, the weight of his accusation crashing down over the celebration.

"What accident?" Alessandro asked, his voice low, his confusion evident.

Enrico turned to face the younger brother, his voice filled with anguish. "Five years ago, my son Luca was working in the vineyard, just like I did. He was exposed to dangerous pesticides—chemicals that should never have been used. Chemicals that your father brought in, ignoring the regulations. Luca was poisoned, and he died. Slowly, painfully."

Emma felt the breath leave her lungs as she listened. This wasn't just a personal grudge—this was a tragedy, one that had been hidden for years. The pieces began to fall into place in her mind: the banned chemicals, Victor's willingness to cut corners to achieve perfection, the resentment of the workers who had been placed in harm's way. Could this be the reason for Victor's murder? Had someone finally taken revenge for the damage he had caused?

"And what did your father do?" Enrico continued, his voice trembling with rage. "He paid us off. Gave us just enough money to keep quiet. He told us to stay silent, that the vineyard couldn't afford a scandal. He covered up my son's death, just like he covered up everything else. And I've had to live with that every day since."

The courtyard was deathly silent now, the festival forgotten, as all eyes turned to Marco. His face had paled, and for a moment, it looked like he was about to deny everything. But something in his expression shifted—perhaps a flicker of guilt, or maybe realization.

"I didn't know," Marco said quietly, his voice hollow. "I didn't know about Luca."

Enrico shook his head, his face twisted with pain. "You didn't want to know. Your father kept you in the dark, just like he kept everyone in the dark. He was so obsessed with his perfect vineyard that he didn't care who he hurt. And now, look what's happened. He's dead. Maybe he finally got what he deserved."

Emma stepped forward, her voice calm but commanding. "Enrico, I'm sorry for your loss. But I need to know more about this. Did anyone else know about the cover-up? Did you ever confront Victor about it?"

Enrico's shoulders sagged as the fight seemed to drain out of him. He glanced down at the ground, shaking his head. "I wanted to confront him. Every day I thought about it. But he was too powerful. No one would listen to me. I was just a worker. He was Victor Castello, the king of the vineyard."

Emma nodded, understanding the deep frustration and helplessness that Enrico must have felt. "And recently? Did anyone else learn the truth? Did you tell anyone?"

Enrico looked up, his eyes filled with bitterness. "Some of the other workers knew. But most of them were too scared to speak up. Marco... he didn't know, but I think he suspected. And Adriana, she kept asking questions. I think she knew something was wrong."

Emma's mind raced. Adriana had been digging into her father's business practices—perhaps she had stumbled upon the truth about the accident. But that didn't explain everything. If Victor had been murdered, it could have been by someone seeking revenge for Luca's death, or it could have been connected to the larger picture of his unethical practices. The pieces were starting to come together, but there was still something missing.

"Enrico," Emma asked, her voice gentle but firm, "did you ever think about confronting Victor directly? About... taking matters into your own hands?"

Enrico looked up at her, his eyes glistening with tears. "I thought about it. Every day I thought about it. But I'm not a killer. I couldn't do it. I couldn't live with more death on my hands."

Emma nodded, believing him. The pain in his voice was raw and real, and while he clearly harboured deep resentment toward Victor, she didn't think he had been the one to end Victor's life. But his revelation had opened a new door in the investigation.

What was left of the crowd began to murmur again, the weight of Enrico's accusations settling over the festival like a dark cloud, Emma knew one thing for certain: Victor Castello had built his empire on lies and deception, and those lies had finally caught up to him.

Someone had killed Victor to protect a secret, to cover up a wrong, or to take revenge for years of suffering. And with the truth about the pesticide accident now out in the open, the stakes had never been higher.

Emma turned her attention back to the Castello family, watching as Marco and Alessandro stood in stunned silence, their world unravelling before them.

DEATH IN THE VINEYARD

The vineyard was crumbling, and so was the Castello name. All that remained was for Emma to uncover who had delivered the final blow.

The truth, it seemed, had a bitter taste.

Chapter 20: The Blind Tasting

The atmosphere at the Castello vineyard had shifted in the days following the Harvest Celebration. The once-celebratory mood had been replaced with tension, as whispers of Victor Castello's dark past spread through the estate. The revelation about Enrico's son and the deadly pesticides had shaken everyone, and now, more than ever, the question loomed: who had killed Victor Castello, and why?

Detective Emma Cross stood at the edge of the vineyard's grand tasting hall, where an exclusive wine-tasting event was set to begin. The event had been planned long before Victor's death, a showcase of the vineyard's finest wines, attended by wealthy investors, critics, and a few high-profile guests. It was a private, invitation-only affair, but Emma had made sure she was on the guest list—after all, this tasting was no ordinary one.

The event had taken on new significance in light of the investigation. Emma had received an anonymous tip earlier that morning, a cryptic message delivered to her hotel: Attend the blind tasting. The answer is in the wine. It had been enough to pique her curiosity, and now, standing in the dimly lit hall filled with elegantly set tables and polished glasses, Emma couldn't shake the feeling that this was where the final pieces of the puzzle would fall into place.

The tasting was being led by one of the vineyard's top sommeliers, a serious-looking man named Antonio who had worked under Victor for years. He moved with precision, carefully pouring the wine into each guest's glass as they whispered in anticipation. Emma took her seat near the back of the room, her eyes scanning the rows of attendees. She spotted Marco near the front, his face tense as he spoke quietly with a few of the vineyard's investors. Alessandro was seated further down, looking equally uneasy.

Adriana sat alone at a small table by the window, her face calm but distant. Emma had noticed a shift in Adriana over the past few days—ever since the revelation of Victor's secrets, she had become quieter, more introspective, as though she were grappling with something deeper than just her family's crumbling legacy.

As the sommelier began introducing the first wine, Emma's attention sharpened. This was no ordinary tasting—it was a "blind tasting," where each wine was served without labels, identified only by its flavour, scent, and texture. The guests were asked to judge the wines based on their senses alone, without the influence of branding or prestige. It was a test of true expertise.

As the first glasses were poured, Emma raised her glass to her nose, inhaling the scent of the wine. It was rich, full-bodied, with hints of oak and berries. But her mind wasn't on the wine itself—it was on the message she had received. The answer is in the wine. What had the tip meant? Was it a reference to the poisoned wine bottle she had found in Victor's office? Was someone trying to point her to the murder weapon?

Emma sipped the wine, allowing the Flavors to settle on her tongue, while keeping an eye on the room. As the sommelier moved on to the second bottle, she noticed something strange. Antonio was pouring the wine with a measured grace, but when he reached a particular bottle, his hands seemed to hesitate. For the briefest moment, his eyes flickered toward Marco, then to Adriana, before he quickly moved on.

Emma's instincts flared. There was something off about that bottle—something Antonio had noticed, even if he hadn't said anything aloud. She watched closely as the sommelier poured the wine into each guest's glass. When he reached Emma's table, he hesitated again, his eyes meeting hers for a fraction of a second before he poured her glass.

The wine was darker than the others, its scent sharper, almost metallic. Emma's heart raced as she lifted the glass, swirling it gently under her nose. There was something familiar about the scent, something that reminded her of the suspicious bottle she had found in Victor's office—the one she suspected had been poisoned.

She took a small sip, allowing the wine to coat her tongue. The flavour was bitter, not in the way a well-aged wine should be, but in a way that sent alarm bells ringing in her mind. This wasn't right. There was something wrong with this wine.

Emma set the glass down and looked around the room. No one else seemed to have noticed anything unusual. The guests were sipping, nodding appreciatively, and murmuring about the flavour profiles, but Emma's focus was elsewhere. Her mind flashed back to the forensic report—the presence of a chemical substance in Victor's bloodstream, one that had been absorbed either through contact or ingestion.

Was this it? Was this wine the key to Victor's death?

Emma discreetly slipped her phone from her pocket and sent a quick message to the forensic team, asking them to prepare for a potential new sample. She needed to confirm her suspicions, but there was no doubt in her mind now: the bottle Antonio had poured from was connected to Victor's murder.

The question was, who had put it there?

As the tasting continued, Emma rose from her seat and quietly made her way toward the back of the room, keeping her eyes on Antonio. She approached him as he finished pouring the final glasses, her voice low but firm.

"Antonio, I need to speak with you," Emma said, catching his attention.

The sommelier glanced around nervously before nodding. He set the bottle down and followed Emma toward a secluded corner of the room.

"What is it, Detective?" Antonio asked, his voice shaky.

Emma didn't waste time. "That last bottle you poured—it wasn't part of the original tasting, was it?"

Antonio's face paled, and he swallowed hard. "No... it wasn't. It was added to the list at the last minute."

"Who added it?" Emma pressed, her eyes narrowing.

"Marco," Antonio admitted, his voice barely a whisper. "He told me it was a special vintage, something his father had been saving. He insisted that it be included in tonight's tasting."

Emma's heart pounded in her chest. Marco. He had been involved in selecting the wines for the event—and now, it seemed, he had introduced a bottle that might very well be the key to solving Victor's murder.

"Antonio," Emma said carefully, "I need you to tell me everything you know about that bottle."

Antonio hesitated, glancing around the room as if afraid someone might overhear. "It was stored in Victor's private collection," he said quietly. "I didn't think much of it at the time, but... when I opened it tonight, something felt off. The scent, the color—it wasn't right."

Emma nodded, her suspicions confirmed. The bottle Marco had added to the tasting was no ordinary vintage—it was the same poisoned wine that had been hidden in Victor's office. But why? Had Marco been involved in his father's death? Or was someone else using the tasting to expose the truth?

Before Emma could ask any more questions, a loud crash echoed through the hall. She spun around to see Marco and Alessandro standing near the tasting table, their faces flushed with anger as they shouted at each other. The tension between them had reached its boiling point, and the crowd was watching in stunned silence.

"You always wanted to control everything!" Alessandro shouted, his voice filled with fury. "But you never cared about this family! You never cared about Father!"

"And you were too weak to stand up to him!" Marco fired back, his fists clenched. "You let him ruin everything!"

Emma's eyes darted between the two brothers, the weight of the investigation bearing down on her. The truth was close, but so was the danger. She knew that whatever secrets had been hidden in the wine were about to come spilling out—and the final reckoning for the Castello family was at hand.

The blind tasting had revealed more than just the flavour of the wine.

It had revealed the bitter truth that had been hidden beneath the surface all along.

The murder weapon had been right in front of them, disguised as the vineyard's finest vintage. And now, with Marco and Alessandro at each other's throats, Emma had to act fast before the vineyard's darkest secrets consumed them all.

The Castello legacy was unravelling, and Emma knew that the final piece of the puzzle was about to fall into place.

Chapter 21: Hidden in the Vines

The Castello vineyard lay in darkness, the rows of vines stretching endlessly into the night like shadowy sentinels guarding their secrets. The only sound was the faint rustle of leaves in the cool breeze as Detective Emma Cross made her way through the vineyard, her flashlight casting long beams of light across the neatly arranged rows. She had come here in the dead of night for a reason—after the revelations at the blind tasting, she knew that the answers she sought wouldn't be found in plain sight. They were hidden somewhere deep in the vineyard, buried in the secrets Victor Castello had taken to his grave.

Emma's mind was racing. The blind tasting had revealed more than just Marco's involvement in selecting the suspicious bottle; it had exposed a deeper, more insidious truth. Someone had tipped her off, guiding her toward the poisoned wine, but that clue had only scratched the surface. There was more to Victor's death—more to his empire—than she had originally thought. And now, as she navigated the dark vineyard, she was closing in on the truth.

Earlier that evening, Emma had confronted Antonio about his knowledge of Victor's private collection. The sommelier had been reluctant at first, but eventually, he had confessed that Victor had been hiding more than just wine in his cellar. Rumours had circulated among the vineyard staff for years—rumours about Victor's involvement in a black-market wine trade, smuggling rare vintages to high-paying buyers under the table. But there was never any proof. Victor had been careful, keeping his illicit dealings well hidden, out of sight of even his most trusted employees.

Until now.

Antonio had pointed her toward the vineyard itself, mentioning that there were areas Victor often visited late at night—areas away from prying eyes. The vineyard was massive, but Emma had a lead: an old storage shed located in a secluded section of the estate. It was a place few people ventured to, and according to Antonio, Victor had been seen there on more than one occasion, always after dark.

Emma approached the shed, her flashlight revealing the weathered wooden structure tucked between two rows of vines. It looked like it hadn't been used for years, its roof sagging and the door hanging slightly ajar. But Emma's instincts told her otherwise. This was where Victor had hidden something—something that could explain his dangerous connections, and maybe even the motive behind his murder.

She stepped inside the shed, her flashlight revealing shelves stacked with old crates and dusty wine barrels. At first glance, it appeared unremarkable—a forgotten storage space filled with discarded vineyard supplies. But Emma knew better. She moved deeper into the shed, her flashlight scanning the walls and floor for any sign of a hidden compartment.

As she inspected the back wall, her hand brushed against a loose panel of wood. Emma paused, her pulse quickening. She pushed against the panel, and it slid away easily, revealing a narrow opening behind it. Inside was a small, hidden compartment, and there, stacked neatly in the dim light, were several thick folders and a metal lockbox.

Emma carefully pulled out the folders and opened the top one. Her heart raced as she scanned the documents inside. They were records—detailed logs of wine shipments, sales, and payments. But these weren't ordinary sales records. The buyers listed in the logs were not the vineyard's usual clientele. These were international contacts—high-end collectors, distributors from countries where wine sales were heavily regulated. And the shipments? They were for rare and vintage wines, some of which had been banned for export due to their value or provenance.

It was exactly what Antonio had hinted at. Victor Castello had been running a black-market wine operation, smuggling rare vintages and selling them to wealthy buyers around the world. The records were meticulous, listing dates, quantities, and payment amounts—all of which pointed to a sophisticated operation that had been in place for years.

Emma's breath caught as she flipped through the pages. Victor had been hiding this side of his business for a long time, laundering money through the vineyard's legitimate operations while using his reputation to conceal the illicit trade. But there was more—Victor had been making substantial profits from these deals, far more than the vineyard's public financial statements suggested. And the payments weren't just for wine. There were notes about "special deliveries" and "private requests," vague terms that hinted at something more sinister.

As Emma reached for the metal lockbox, her fingers trembling slightly, she knew this was the key to Victor's murder. Whoever had killed him had likely discovered his secret dealings or been involved in them. The black-market trade had made Victor powerful—and vulnerable.

She tried the lockbox, but it was sealed tight. Emma pulled a small set of tools from her bag and quickly picked the lock, her years of investigative work coming in handy. The box clicked open, and inside, she found several bundles of cash and more documents, but one in particular stood out—a contract, signed by Victor, detailing a massive deal with an unnamed buyer. The terms of the deal were staggering, involving the sale of a collection of rare vintages worth millions. But it wasn't the sale itself that caught Emma's attention—it was the clause at the bottom.

This agreement is contingent upon the delivery of the specified wines by the end of the current harvest. Failure to meet this deadline will result in legal and financial penalties, as well as the immediate forfeiture of Castello Vineyards' assets.

Emma's heart pounded as she realized what this meant. Victor had been under immense pressure to deliver the wines—wines that may not have even existed in the quantities promised. And if he failed, he stood to lose everything. Could this deal have been the motive for his murder? Had someone killed him to cover up the fact that the vineyard was on the brink of collapse?

As Emma gathered the documents, a sound outside the shed caught her attention—a soft rustling in the vines. She froze, her hand instinctively going to her side where her gun was holstered. Someone was out there, watching her.

She quickly slipped the documents into her bag and turned off her flashlight, plunging the shed into darkness. The rustling grew louder, and she could hear the faint sound of footsteps approaching the shed.

Emma's mind raced. Had someone followed her here? Or had they been watching the shed, waiting for her to uncover what Victor had hidden? Whoever it was, they didn't want these documents to see the light of day.

The footsteps stopped just outside the door, and Emma held her breath, her heart pounding in her chest. She could hear the soft creak of the wooden floorboards as someone stepped inside the shed. In the darkness, she saw the faint outline of a figure, their movements cautious and deliberate.

Emma waited, watching the figure as they moved closer to the back wall. She didn't know who they were yet, but she wasn't going to wait to find out. In one swift motion, she stepped forward, turning on her flashlight and shining it directly at the intruder's face.

"Stop right there," Emma commanded, her voice steady.

The figure froze, momentarily blinded by the light. As the beam illuminated their face, Emma's stomach dropped.

It was Marco Castello.

His face was pale, his eyes wide with shock as he stared at Emma. He looked like he had been caught red-handed, but his expression quickly shifted to anger.

"What are you doing here?" Marco demanded, his voice tense. "This is my family's property."

"I could ask you the same question," Emma replied, keeping the flashlight trained on him. "You were looking for something, weren't you? Something your father kept hidden here."

Marco's jaw clenched, and for a moment, he said nothing. Then, in a low voice, he muttered, "I knew there was something. I knew he was hiding things from us. But I didn't know it was this bad."

Emma stepped closer, her eyes narrowing. "You knew about the black-market deals, didn't you? That your father was using the vineyard to smuggle rare wines?"

Marco's face twisted with frustration. "I suspected it. But he never let me in on the details. I wasn't... trusted. Not with the real secrets."

Emma lowered the flashlight slightly, studying Marco's face. He looked genuinely conflicted, torn between anger and guilt.

"Did you know about this contract?" Emma asked, pulling out the document she had found in the lockbox. "Victor was under pressure to deliver by the end of this harvest. He stood to lose everything if he didn't."

Marco stared at the document, his expression darkening. "No... I didn't know about that."

Emma's mind raced. If Marco hadn't known about the contract, then maybe he wasn't directly involved in the black-market trade. But someone else had known—someone who had killed Victor to protect these secrets. And now, standing in the darkness of the vineyard, Emma realized that the truth was finally within her grasp.

Victor's secrets had been hidden in the vines, but now they were exposed.

And the killer was closer than ever.

Chapter 22: A Bitter Blend

The morning sun had just begun to cast its warm glow over the Castello vineyard, illuminating the rows of vines in a golden light. But Detective Emma Cross had no time to enjoy the peaceful scene. The discovery she'd made in the hidden storage shed the night before—Victor Castello's secret involvement in a black-market wine trade—had shifted the investigation into high gear. Now, a new lead had emerged, and it was taking Emma into even murkier territory.

Luca Rossi.

The Rossi family, long-time rivals of the Castellos, had been hovering on the edge of suspicion since the beginning of the investigation. The feud between the two families was legendary, their competition in the wine business fierce and often bitter. But despite their animosity, there had been little evidence directly linking Luca or his family to Victor's death. Until now.

Early that morning, Emma had received an anonymous tip—another in the string of cryptic messages that seemed to be guiding her investigation. This time, it had been more specific: Luca Rossi has been bribing a vineyard worker for secrets about Victor's wine production. Meet them at the east side of the vineyard. Tonight.

If Luca had been trying to undermine Victor's business, it could explain a motive for sabotage, maybe even for murder. But bribery didn't make him a killer. Emma needed to see for herself what was going on—and whether Luca Rossi was more deeply involved in Victor's death than she had first thought.

As dusk settled over the vineyard, Emma made her way to the east side, a more secluded area near the edge of the property where few workers ventured after dark. The vines here were dense, the rows long and winding. It was the perfect place for a secret meeting. Emma moved carefully through the vines, keeping to the shadows as she approached the spot where the tip had directed her.

She spotted them easily enough—a tall, broad figure that could only be Luca Rossi, and another man, a vineyard worker she didn't recognize, standing nervously in front of him. They were huddled together, speaking in low voices, the tension between them palpable.

Emma edged closer, careful not to make a sound. She positioned herself behind a nearby row of vines, close enough to hear their conversation but hidden from view.

"I told you everything I know," the worker said, his voice shaking slightly. "I can't keep doing this. If they find out—"

"They won't," Luca snapped, his voice low but sharp. "You're getting paid well, aren't you? All I need is a little more information. I want to know how Victor was producing that last vintage. The formula, the process—everything."

The worker hesitated, glancing around nervously. "I don't have access to that kind of information. Only Marco and a few others worked directly with Victor on the last vintage."

"You're lying," Luca growled, stepping closer. "You've been working at the vineyard for years. You know more than you're letting on. I need those secrets, and you're going to get them for me."

The worker's eyes darted around, his fear growing more apparent. "Please, I—"

Before he could finish, Luca reached into his jacket and pulled out an envelope, shoving it into the worker's hands. "Take this. It's more than enough to buy your silence. But don't think for a second that you can walk away from this. I want answers, and I'll get them one way or another."

The worker swallowed hard, clutching the envelope with trembling hands. He nodded quickly, his eyes wide with fear.

Satisfied, Luca turned on his heel and began to walk away, leaving the worker standing there, visibly shaken. Emma watched him for a moment before making her move.

"Luca!" she called out, stepping out from behind the vines.

Luca froze, then slowly turned around, his face hardening when he saw her. "Detective Cross," he said coolly, his voice dripping with disdain. "To what do I owe this pleasure?"

Emma walked toward him, her eyes sharp. "I'd like to ask you the same question. What are you doing bribing one of the vineyard workers for information about Victor's wine production?"

Luca's jaw tightened, but he kept his expression neutral. "I don't know what you're talking about."

"Save it, Luca. I heard everything," Emma said, stepping closer. "You've been trying to get your hands on the formula for Victor's last vintage. Why? What's so important about it?"

Luca's eyes flashed with anger. "What's important is that Victor was hiding something. His last vintage was supposed to be revolutionary, and yet no one knew what he was doing. I wanted to find out how he was producing it, how he was going to surpass the Rossi name once and for all."

"So you've been paying off workers to steal secrets from the Castello vineyard?" Emma asked, her tone sharp. "That's a dangerous game, Luca."

Luca crossed his arms, his expression defiant. "Victor played dirty for years. Don't act like I'm the villain here, Detective. He was just as ruthless, if not worse. I wasn't going to let him destroy the Rossi family's reputation with whatever scheme he was pulling."

Emma studied him, her mind racing. Luca's bitterness toward Victor was undeniable, but was it enough to drive him to murder? Was his need to protect the Rossi name so great that he would have killed Victor to stop him?

"Is that why you killed him?" Emma asked bluntly, watching Luca's reaction carefully.

Luca's eyes widened for a fraction of a second, but he quickly recovered, his face hardening into a mask of anger. "I didn't kill him.

I wanted answers, yes. I wanted to protect my family's legacy. But murder? No. That's not how I do business."

Emma held his gaze, searching for any sign of deception. Luca was a smooth operator, and while his rivalry with Victor was real, she couldn't shake the feeling that there was more to the story.

"You bribed this worker to get information about the last vintage," Emma said, her voice steady. "But what if there was something more at stake? Something bigger than just a new wine formula?"

Luca's eyes flickered with something—fear, perhaps, or recognition. "What are you getting at?"

Emma took a step closer, her voice lowering. "Victor was involved in a black-market wine trade. He was smuggling rare vintages, making millions off of illicit deals. Someone found out about it, and now he's dead. So tell me, Luca—how deep were you in?"

Luca's face drained of color, and for the first time, Emma saw real panic in his eyes. "I didn't know about that. I swear."

Emma narrowed her eyes. "But you knew Victor was hiding something, didn't you? You knew there was more going on at Castello Vineyards than just wine production."

Luca said nothing, his silence speaking volumes.

Emma took a deep breath, piecing it all together. Luca had been desperate to protect the Rossi name, to keep the Castello family from overtaking his own. But while his rivalry with Victor had pushed him to bribe vineyard workers and steal secrets, it didn't make him a killer. The real motive for murder lay deeper, in the shadows of Victor's black-market dealings. And someone—perhaps more than one person—had wanted those secrets buried for good.

"You're not off the hook yet, Luca," Emma said, her voice firm. "But I believe you. You didn't kill Victor. You just wanted to protect your family's reputation."

Luca's shoulders sagged with relief, but the tension between them remained. "So what now?"

Emma glanced at the frightened vineyard worker, still standing frozen with the envelope in his hand. "You go home, and you stop bribing people for secrets. I'll be in touch if I have more questions."

Luca nodded, his face grim, before turning and walking away into the night. Emma watched him go, her mind still churning with unanswered questions.

Luca Rossi might not have been the murderer, but he was a piece of the puzzle—another thread in the tangled web of greed, rivalry, and betrayal that surrounded Victor's death.

As the vineyard fell silent once more, Emma knew the truth was still hidden in the vines.

And it was only a matter of time before the killer revealed themselves.

Chapter 23: Family Ties

Detective Emma Cross had seen enough family secrets unravel over the course of her investigation at Castello Vineyards to know that the truth was rarely what it seemed. Yet even she was unprepared for the bombshell she was about to uncover. The Castello family, already divided by power struggles, greed, and ambition, was about to be shaken to its very core.

It had all started with an anonymous letter.

The envelope had arrived at her temporary office that morning, unmarked except for her name scrawled hastily on the front. Inside was a single sheet of paper with a message that made her stomach drop: There's one more heir. The child Victor kept hidden could change everything.

Emma had been chasing clues about Victor's dark dealings, uncovering secrets that threatened to tear the vineyard apart. But this? This was something she hadn't anticipated. An illegitimate child meant that the entire balance of power in the Castello family could shift. If this child had a rightful claim to the vineyard, the stakes were higher than she could have imagined.

The letter included an address—a small apartment in the nearby village—and instructions to meet someone there that evening. Emma wasn't sure who had sent the note, but she knew she had to follow the lead. If Victor had kept this child a secret, it was possible that no one else in the family knew. And if this secret was tied to his murder, then the Castello legacy was in even greater danger than she'd realized.

That evening, Emma arrived at the address, a modest building tucked away on a quiet street. The village felt eerily still, and the fading light of dusk cast long shadows across the cobblestones. She approached the door and knocked softly, her heart racing as she wondered who—or what—she would find on the other side.

The door creaked open a moment later, and a woman in her early thirties stood before her. She had dark hair and striking features, her eyes sharp with intelligence but clouded with a hint of unease. She didn't invite Emma in immediately, instead studying her with a wary expression.

"You must be Detective Cross," the woman said, her voice quiet but steady. "Come in. I've been expecting you."

Emma stepped inside, her mind racing with questions. The apartment was simple, with minimal furniture and a few personal items scattered about. It didn't feel like a permanent home—more like a place to hide.

The woman gestured for Emma to sit, taking a seat herself across from her. "I'm Sofia," she said, her eyes not leaving Emma's. "I assume you're here because of the letter."

Emma nodded, her gaze steady. "Yes. I was told Victor Castello had an illegitimate child. Is that you?"

Sofia let out a small, bitter laugh, shaking her head. "No, it's not me. But you're close." She hesitated, then leaned forward, lowering her voice. "I'm the mother."

Emma's heart skipped a beat. This was the last thing she had expected. "So Victor had a child with you? And he kept it hidden?"

Sofia nodded, her expression hardening. "Yes. His name is Luca. He's eight years old now. Victor made sure no one knew about him—not his family, not his business associates. He was terrified of what would happen if the truth came out."

Emma leaned forward, her mind working rapidly to process this new information. "Why did he keep Luca a secret? Was it just about protecting his reputation, or was there something more?"

Sofia's eyes darkened. "It was about power. Victor knew that if his family found out about Luca, it would cause chaos. The vineyard is everything to the Castello family. If Luca's existence had come to light, it would have thrown everything into question—especially who would inherit the vineyard."

Emma's thoughts raced. An illegitimate child could indeed upend the entire balance of power in the family. Marco and Alessandro had been battling for control of the vineyard ever since Victor's death, but if Luca had a rightful claim, it could strip them of their positions entirely. And if Adriana found out? Her ambitions for control would be dashed in an instant.

"Why are you telling me this now?" Emma asked, her voice steady but filled with curiosity. "Why didn't you come forward earlier?"

Sofia looked away, her expression pained. "I didn't want to expose Luca to the madness of the Castello family. Victor paid me to stay silent, to raise Luca away from the vineyard. I agreed, because I thought it was best for my son. But after Victor's death... things have changed. I'm afraid for Luca's future."

Emma's mind churned. Victor's death had created a power vacuum, and Luca's existence could either complicate the battle for control—or offer a solution. But there was something else nagging at her.

"Do you think someone in the family found out about Luca?" Emma asked carefully. "Could that have been a motive for Victor's murder?"

Sofia's face tightened. "I don't know. I thought we were careful, but Victor was growing more paranoid in the months before his death. He kept talking about how the vineyard was at risk, how everything could fall apart if he didn't secure it before it was too late. He never mentioned Luca directly, but I could tell something was weighing on him."

Emma considered this. If someone had learned about Luca and believed that the child threatened their inheritance or control over the vineyard, it could provide a powerful motive for murder. But who would have discovered the secret? And more importantly, how far would they go to protect their claim?

"I need to know more," Emma said, her voice firm but compassionate. "Is there anything else you can tell me? Did Victor ever hint that someone might be onto him?"

Sofia shook her head, looking frustrated. "No. But I know this—Victor was planning something big before he died. He was obsessed with his last vintage, yes, but there was more to it. He was trying to protect the vineyard for Luca, even if he couldn't acknowledge him publicly. That's why he made some of those shady deals, I'm sure of it."

Emma's pulse quickened. If Victor had been trying to secure the vineyard for his secret child, it explained a lot about his desperation in those final months. But it also meant that someone in the Castello family could have seen Luca as a threat—and acted accordingly.

Sofia leaned forward, her eyes pleading. "I don't want my son dragged into this mess, Detective. But I'm telling you this because I think someone in the family may have found out. And if they did..."

Emma nodded slowly, understanding the weight of Sofia's fears. "If they did, it could have cost Victor his life."

The room fell silent as the gravity of the situation settled between them. Emma now had to consider a new angle in the investigation—one that involved not just business and legacy, but family secrets, betrayal, and a child whose very existence could change everything.

As she left the apartment, the night air cool against her skin, Emma's thoughts whirled. The battle for control of Castello Vineyards was more complex than she had ever imagined. And now, with the revelation of Victor's illegitimate child, the stakes had never been higher.

Someone had killed Victor Castello to protect their claim to the vineyard. And whoever it was, they weren't done fighting yet.

The final showdown was coming, and Emma knew that the truth about Luca could shift the entire balance of power in the Castello family.

Family ties, it seemed, were more dangerous than ever.

Part 5: Decanting the Truth
Chapter 24: Tainted Legacy

The Castello vineyard, with its endless rows of meticulously maintained vines, was more than just a business—it was the embodiment of Victor Castello's legacy. It represented years of hard work, cunning deals, and a relentless pursuit of power. But Detective Emma Cross had come to realize that beneath the vineyard's polished surface, a darker truth was buried, a truth that stretched far beyond the secrets of Victor's black-market dealings or his illegitimate child.

As Emma delved deeper into Victor's past, she uncovered another layer to the complex web of motives surrounding his murder. It wasn't just about the vineyard's future or the family's struggle for control—it was about the land itself. A land dispute, long hidden and potentially lethal, had surfaced as a possible motive for Victor's death.

It had started with an innocuous lead—a dusty old file that Emma had found while combing through Victor's personal documents. The file was tucked away in the back of a drawer in his private office, marked only with the name "D'Amato." The name meant nothing to Emma at first, but as she began to investigate, she realized it belonged to a neighbouring family with deep roots in the region. The D'Amatos had once owned a portion of the land where Castello Vineyards now stood.

But something had happened between the Castellos and the D'Amatos. The documents in the file hinted at a bitter dispute over land ownership that had escalated decades ago. Victor had managed to acquire the D'Amatos' land through questionable means, but it seemed the fight hadn't ended there.

Emma had to know more. She reached out to a local historian, an elderly man named Signor Bianchi, who had lived in the area his entire life and knew the histories of all the families. When they met at a small café in the village, Signor Bianchi greeted her with a knowing smile.

"I've heard you've been asking about the D'Amato family," Bianchi said, his voice raspy but warm. "It's a name that brings back memories of bad blood, I'm afraid."

Emma leaned forward, intrigued. "What happened between them and the Castello family? I found some documents that suggest a land dispute."

Signor Bianchi sighed, shaking his head. "Ah, the land... it always comes back to the land, doesn't it? Yes, there was a dispute—a serious one. The D'Amatos once owned a large portion of what is now Castello Vineyards. They were winemakers too, but their family wasn't as wealthy or as powerful as the Castellos. Victor wanted their land. He saw an opportunity to expand, and he took it."

Emma's brow furrowed. "How? Did he buy it outright?"

Bianchi's eyes darkened. "Not exactly. It was a clever play. The D'Amatos had fallen on hard times, financially. Victor offered them what seemed like a fair price, but it wasn't enough to keep them afloat. He knew they were desperate. When the D'Amatos refused to sell outright, Victor found another way—he manipulated legal loopholes, pressured them with debt, and eventually forced them off the land."

Emma's stomach twisted. "So Victor essentially stole the land from them?"

"In a way, yes," Bianchi replied, his expression grim. "The D'Amato family never forgave him for it. There were threats, accusations, even a few violent encounters between the two families. But Victor was untouchable. The law sided with him, as it often does with those who have power and money."

Emma's mind raced. This was a significant revelation. A land dispute that had left a family bitter and vengeful—this was more than just a business rivalry. This was deeply personal.

"What happened to the D'Amato family after they lost the land?" Emma asked, sensing there was more to the story.

Bianchi sighed again, his gaze distant. "They never recovered. The patriarch, Carlo D'Amato, died a few years later—some say from a broken heart. His son, Giulio, tried to keep the family business afloat, but without the land, it was impossible. Giulio grew bitter, angry. The D'Amatos moved away, but they never forgot what Victor had done."

Emma leaned back in her chair, the pieces starting to come together. The D'Amatos had lost everything because of Victor's ruthless ambition. And now, decades later, the bitterness and resentment might have resurfaced, providing a motive for revenge.

"Do you know where Giulio is now?" Emma asked. "Is there any chance he could be connected to Victor's death?"

Bianchi nodded slowly. "Giulio came back to the village a few years ago. He lives quietly on the outskirts, but I've heard he still harbours a lot of anger toward the Castello family. If you're looking for someone with a motive, Detective, you may want to start with him."

Emma thanked Signor Bianchi for his help and left the café, her mind swirling with new possibilities. If Giulio D'Amato had returned, carrying the weight of his family's loss and hatred for the Castello name, he could have seen Victor's death as a way to finally avenge the wrongs done to his family. But had Giulio been involved in the murder? Or was this just another piece of the larger puzzle?

Later that evening, Emma drove to the outskirts of the village, where Giulio D'Amato was rumoured to live. The road was narrow and winding, the countryside dark and quiet as the vineyard's influence faded behind her. She eventually came to a small, weathered house set back from the road, surrounded by overgrown fields and trees that seemed to press in on the property.

Emma parked her car and approached the house, her footsteps crunching on the gravel. The lights were dim inside, and for a moment, she wondered if anyone was home. She knocked on the door, and after a long pause, it opened a crack.

An older man stood on the other side, his face lined with age and hardship. His eyes were sharp, though, and Emma could see the remnants of the bitterness that had shaped his life. This had to be Giulio D'Amato.

"Are you Giulio D'Amato?" Emma asked, keeping her voice calm.

The man's eyes narrowed, and he gave a curt nod. "Who's asking?"

"I'm Detective Cross. I'm investigating the death of Victor Castello."

Giulio's expression darkened instantly, his lips curling into a sneer. "Victor Castello," he spat, as if the name left a bad taste in his mouth. "What do I care if that man is dead?"

Emma met his gaze, her instincts telling her to proceed carefully. "I know about the history between your family and the Castellos. The land dispute, how Victor forced your family off the property."

Giulio's face twisted with anger. "He ruined us," he said bitterly. "My father worked that land for generations, and Victor stole it from us. He destroyed our family. And now, after all these years, he's finally dead? Good riddance."

Emma's heart raced, but she kept her voice steady. "Did you kill him, Giulio? Did you take revenge on Victor for what he did to your family?"

Giulio's eyes flashed with fury, but then he let out a bitter laugh. "Kill him? No. If I wanted Victor dead, I would've done it years ago, when I had the chance. But I didn't need to. The man was already dead inside. His greed, his ambition—it ate him alive."

Emma studied him, searching for any sign of deceit. Giulio's anger was palpable, but it didn't feel like the anger of a man who had murdered in cold blood. It felt like the anger of someone who had already lost everything—and had nothing left to lose.

"If you didn't kill him, then who did?" Emma pressed.

Giulio shook his head, his voice low and tired. "I don't know. But whoever it was, they did the world a favour. Victor Castello was a man who destroyed everything he touched, including my family's legacy. And now, the same thing is happening to his."

As Emma left Giulio's house and drove back toward the vineyard, she couldn't shake the feeling that Giulio had been telling the truth. He hadn't killed Victor—but he had made it clear that Victor's enemies were many, and the impact of his ruthless business practices had left deep scars on more than just his family.

The land dispute was yet another thread in the tangled web of motives surrounding Victor's death. Someone had killed Victor to protect their interests, to settle old scores, or to ensure control over the vineyard's future.

But as Emma neared the vineyard, one thing became clear: Victor Castello's legacy was tainted, and that taint had spread far beyond the borders of the vineyard.

The truth, like the vines themselves, was twisted and hidden deep within the soil.

And Emma was getting closer to unearthing it.

Chapter 25: Vintage Secrets

The Castello vineyard was bathed in the soft light of the late afternoon sun, casting long shadows across the vines. It had been a tumultuous few weeks for the vineyard, with secrets unearthed, family tensions boiling over, and the once-proud legacy of Victor Castello slowly unravelling. But Detective Emma Cross knew there was still one mystery that remained unresolved—Victor's final vintage.

Victor's obsession with the last vintage had been at the heart of everything. He had poured his life into crafting what he believed would be his greatest achievement, a wine that would secure the Castello name for generations to come. But as Emma dug deeper into the vineyard's secrets, she began to suspect that this final vintage might hold the key to understanding Victor's death.

Emma had arranged a meeting with Lorenzo Bianchi, the vineyard's master winemaker. Lorenzo had worked at Castello Vineyards for decades, earning a reputation as one of the most talented and meticulous winemakers in the region. He had been Victor's trusted right-hand man in the wine production process, and Emma hoped that he could shed some light on what had really been happening in the vineyard during those final months before Victor's death.

The winemaker's cottage sat at the edge of the vineyard, tucked away from the main estate. Emma knocked on the door, and after a moment, it swung open. Lorenzo stood before her, a tall man in his sixties with weathered skin and deep-set eyes that spoke of years of experience and quiet observation.

"Detective Cross," Lorenzo greeted her, his voice rough but kind. "I've been expecting you."

Emma nodded, stepping inside. The cottage was simple, with shelves filled with books on winemaking and bottles of wine lining the walls. The smell of oak and earth filled the air. Lorenzo gestured for her to sit at a small wooden table by the window, and as she did, he poured them each a glass of wine.

"I'm guessing you didn't come here just for a tasting," Lorenzo said, offering a faint smile.

Emma returned the smile but quickly got to the point. "No, I'm here because of Victor's final vintage. There's been a lot of speculation about it—about what made it so special, and why Victor was so obsessed with it. I need to know what you know, Lorenzo. Was there something unusual about that vintage?"

Lorenzo's face grew serious as he sat down across from her. He took a sip of his wine before answering, his eyes distant, as though recalling memories he'd tried to bury.

"Victor's final vintage was supposed to be his masterpiece," Lorenzo began. "He was always a perfectionist, but this time... it was different. He was more secretive, more controlling than I'd ever seen him. He kept the process almost entirely to himself. Only a handful of us were allowed to work on it."

Emma leaned in slightly, her interest piqued. "What made it so special?"

Lorenzo sighed, setting his glass down. "Victor was experimenting with a new blend, using grapes from specific sections of the vineyard—sections that he believed produced the best flavour profiles. He was using techniques that were unorthodox, pushing the limits of what we usually did. The idea was to create something no one had ever tasted before. But there was more to it."

Emma frowned. "More? What do you mean?"

Lorenzo hesitated, his expression conflicted. "There were... whispers among the workers. Whispers that someone had tampered with the vintage. At first, I didn't believe it. But as the harvest went on, I started noticing things—small things that seemed off. Barrels that had been moved, fermentation times that didn't match what I had logged. I confronted Victor about it, but he brushed me off. Said everything was under control."

Emma's pulse quickened. "Do you think someone sabotaged the vintage?"

Lorenzo met her gaze, his voice low and troubled. "Yes. I'm certain of it now. The final batch—the one Victor was most proud of—had been tampered with. I don't know exactly how, but I know the wine wasn't what it was supposed to be. Victor was too focused on the end result, too driven by his need to make this vintage perfect. He didn't see what was happening right under his nose."

Emma's mind raced as she considered the implications. Victor's final vintage had been the culmination of years of work, a project he had poured his soul into. If someone had sabotaged it, they would have had a powerful motive. Not only would it ruin Victor's reputation, but it could also destroy the vineyard's future.

"Who had access to the vintage?" Emma asked, her voice steady. "Who could have tampered with it?"

Lorenzo shook his head, frustration etched into his features. "That's the thing—very few people had access to the cellar where the vintage was being stored. Myself, Marco, Alessandro on occasion, and a few trusted workers. Victor kept everything locked down tight. Whoever tampered with it must have known exactly what they were doing."

Emma thought of the rivalry between Marco and Alessandro, the tension that had been brewing for years. Could one of them have sabotaged the vintage in an attempt to undermine Victor—or each other? Or was there someone else involved, someone with a different motive?

"Why would anyone want to sabotage the wine?" Emma asked, probing deeper. "What would they gain from it?"

Lorenzo leaned back in his chair, rubbing a hand over his tired eyes. "I've been asking myself that same question. It could have been jealousy, a power play within the family. But I think there's more to it. Victor was involved in some dangerous deals toward the end. He was desperate to make sure the vineyard succeeded, no matter the cost. I wouldn't be surprised if someone sabotaged the vintage to ruin him—financially or otherwise."

Emma nodded, her mind churning with possibilities. Victor's black-market wine trade, the secret land dispute, and now the sabotage of his final vintage—it was all connected, each thread weaving together into a larger, more dangerous plot. The stakes were higher than just family rivalry. Someone had wanted to destroy Victor's legacy, and they had been willing to go to great lengths to do it.

"Do you think Victor knew the wine had been sabotaged?" Emma asked quietly.

Lorenzo's eyes darkened. "I don't know. He was so focused on making the vintage perfect that he might not have seen it. Or maybe he did, and he thought he could fix it before anyone else found out."

Emma took a deep breath, the weight of the investigation pressing down on her. "And what about after Victor's death? What happened to the vintage?"

Lorenzo looked away, a pained expression crossing his face. "It's still in the cellar. No one's touched it since Victor died. The family's been too busy fighting over control of the vineyard to even think about the wine."

Emma stood, her resolve hardening. "I need to see that vintage, Lorenzo. If it was tampered with, it could be the key to understanding what really happened to Victor."

Lorenzo nodded slowly. "I'll take you there. But be careful, Detective. This vintage... it's more than just wine. It's the last piece of Victor's legacy. And if someone was willing to kill him to protect their secret, they won't hesitate to do it again."

The cellar was cool and dark, the air thick with the scent of aging wine and oak. Emma followed Lorenzo down the narrow stone steps, her flashlight casting long shadows on the walls. They reached the bottom, where rows of barrels and bottles were stored, each one meticulously labelled.

"This is it," Lorenzo said, stopping in front of a large oak barrel. "The last vintage."

Emma stepped forward, her heart pounding as she ran her fingers over the barrel's surface. This was the wine that Victor had believed would secure his family's future—the wine that had been tampered with, possibly ruined. And it was the wine that might hold the key to his murder.

Lorenzo handed Emma a small tool to tap the barrel, allowing her to sample the wine. She filled a glass and swirled it, bringing it to her nose. The scent was rich, but there was something off—something subtle, yet unmistakable.

She took a small sip, and her suspicions were confirmed. The wine had been altered, its taste tainted by something unnatural. It wasn't just a matter of poor winemaking—this had been deliberate.

Someone had sabotaged Victor's final vintage, and in doing so, they had set the wheels in motion for his death.

As Emma stood in the cool cellar, holding the glass of tainted wine in her hand, she knew the truth was close. The sabotage, the black-market deals, the bitter rivalries—they were all part of the same tangled web. And soon, she would unravel it.

Victor Castello's final vintage had been his downfall.

And whoever had orchestrated the sabotage was still out there, waiting to claim their victory.

But Emma was determined to stop them before they could strike again.

Chapter 26: The Broken Vine

The tension in the Castello family had been simmering for weeks, and Detective Emma Cross knew it was only a matter of time before it reached a boiling point. Secrets had been exposed, alliances had shifted, and the revelation of Victor Castello's dark dealings had left the family teetering on the edge of collapse. But no one could have predicted just how far the family would fracture—or how quickly everything would spiral into violence.

Emma had been invited to attend a family meeting at the Castello estate, a rare gathering where Marco, Alessandro, and Adriana would finally discuss the future of the vineyard. Emma had hoped that this meeting might bring some resolution, or at least offer her a clearer picture of who might have been involved in Victor's death. But as she walked into the grand sitting room, she could sense that something wasn't right.

The room was filled with an uneasy silence, the kind that comes before a storm. Marco stood near the fireplace, his broad shoulders tense, his face set in a hard expression. Alessandro leaned against the far wall, arms crossed, his eyes flickering with barely concealed anger. Adriana sat in the center of the room, her posture stiff, her eyes cold and calculating as she watched her brothers.

Emma took a seat in a corner, observing the dynamics at play. The air in the room was thick with unspoken grievances, old resentments, and the weight of recent discoveries. Each of them had something to lose—and everything to gain.

Marco was the first to speak, his voice tight with frustration. "We need to come to an agreement about the vineyard. This fighting between us has to end."

Alessandro scoffed, his expression mocking. "Now you want to make peace? After you've done everything to sabotage me? You've always wanted control of the vineyard, Marco. Don't pretend like you care about anything else."

Marco's jaw clenched, his fists tightening at his sides. "I've been trying to save this vineyard from falling apart, Alessandro. If you had been more involved, maybe you'd understand the pressure I've been under."

Adriana's voice cut through the room, sharp and cold. "Both of you need to stop pretending like you're the only ones who care about this family. The vineyard is falling apart because of Father's secrets, not because of either of you. And now, we're all paying the price for his mistakes."

Emma's eyes darted between them, watching the way the tension built with each word. The Castello family was unravelling, and it was clear that the cracks in their relationships had been there long before Victor's death.

Alessandro pushed away from the wall, his voice rising in anger. "Father's mistakes? Or maybe it's yours, Adriana. You've been angling for control since the beginning. Always trying to position yourself as the smart one, the one who should be running everything. Maybe you're the one who sabotaged the vintage."

Adriana's eyes flashed with fury, and she stood, her voice low and dangerous. "Don't you dare accuse me of that, Alessandro. I've worked harder than both of you to keep this family together. I've been the one cleaning up your messes, covering for you when you couldn't handle Father's expectations."

Marco took a step forward, his voice booming as he spoke. "Enough! This isn't about who's to blame. It's about what we're going to do now. We need to make a decision before the vineyard falls apart completely."

Adriana turned her cold gaze to Marco. "The only reason the vineyard is in danger is because you've been hiding things from us. The black-market deals, the illegal practices—it's all come back to haunt us because of your decisions."

Marco's face flushed with anger. "I didn't make those deals, Adriana. That was Father. He kept me in the dark about half of what he was doing."

Alessandro sneered. "Oh, please. You were his golden boy. Of course, you knew what he was doing. You were just too spineless to stand up to him."

The room was charged with hostility, the bitterness between the siblings spilling over. Emma could feel the situation escalating, and she knew she had to intervene before it turned physical.

"Stop," Emma said, her voice firm but calm. "This isn't helping any of you. If you keep tearing each other apart, the vineyard will be the least of your concerns. You need to focus on what really matters—finding out who killed your father."

But her words fell on deaf ears.

Adriana turned on Marco, her voice trembling with rage. "You've always wanted to control everything, Marco. Just like Father. You think you can run this vineyard on your own, but you're not strong enough. You never were."

Marco's eyes blazed with fury. "You have no idea what I've been through, Adriana. No idea what I've sacrificed to keep this family together."

Alessandro stepped forward, his voice dripping with venom. "Sacrificed? Don't make me laugh. You've done nothing but look out for yourself. And now, you're going to pay for it."

In one swift motion, Alessandro lunged at Marco, shoving him hard in the chest. Marco stumbled back, crashing into the side table, sending a bottle of wine shattering to the floor. The sharp sound echoed through the room, but it didn't stop the two brothers from grappling with each other, their rage finally boiling over.

"Enough!" Emma shouted, stepping forward to try and separate them.

But before she could reach them, the situation exploded.

Adriana, her face twisted with fury, grabbed the broken neck of the wine bottle from the floor and swung it toward Alessandro, her voice a scream of pent-up rage. "I won't let you destroy this family!"

Alessandro barely managed to dodge the attack, the jagged glass grazing his arm. Blood bloomed across his sleeve as he recoiled, his eyes wide with shock and anger.

"Adriana!" Marco shouted, pulling her back before she could strike again.

The room descended into chaos. Alessandro, clutching his wounded arm, glared at Adriana with a mixture of rage and fear. Marco stood between them, his chest heaving as he struggled to keep control. And Adriana, her face pale and trembling, dropped the broken bottle to the floor, the realization of what she had just done settling in.

Emma rushed forward, her heart pounding. "Everyone, stop! This isn't going to solve anything."

But the damage had been done. The Castello family had finally broken, their fragile ties shattered in a moment of violence.

As Emma looked around the room, she knew that this fight wasn't just about the vineyard—it was about years of betrayal, jealousy, and unresolved pain. Victor's death had been the spark that ignited the fire, but the flames had been smouldering for years.

"Sit down," Emma commanded, her voice sharp. "We're not leaving this room until we figure out what's really going on. Enough secrets. Enough lies."

Adriana, her hands shaking, collapsed into a chair, her eyes vacant and haunted. Alessandro sat down across from her, his hand still pressed to his bleeding arm, glaring at his sister. And Marco stood in the center of the room, his face filled with a mix of anger and helplessness.

Emma took a deep breath, gathering her thoughts. The Castello family had reached their breaking point, but the truth was still out there—hidden in the tangled web of lies and betrayals.

"Victor's death has torn this family apart," Emma said quietly, her voice steady. "But before any of you can move forward, we need to uncover the real motive for his murder."

As the room fell into an uneasy silence, Emma knew that the answers were closer than ever.

But the Castello family's broken ties had left scars that might never heal.

And the vineyard—Victor's legacy—might never recover from the violence that had just erupted within its walls.

Chapter 27: Pressing for Answers

The tension in the Castello household had reached its peak. Emma Cross had witnessed the family's violent breakdown firsthand, and now the threads of Victor Castello's life were unravelling faster than she could piece them together. With every step deeper into the investigation, she uncovered new layers of secrets—each more dangerous than the last. But the answers she needed were still elusive.

One name kept surfacing during her investigation: Isabela, Victor's widow. While the rest of the family had been caught up in power struggles and bitter rivalries, Isabela had remained quiet, keeping a low profile. Too quiet, Emma thought. She had been reluctant to press Isabela in the earlier stages of the investigation, but now, with the vineyard's future at stake and the family tearing itself apart, Emma knew she had no choice but to confront her.

Isabela Castello, once the matriarch of the family, had always been a poised and calculating woman. She had played her role well—silent, dignified, and seemingly uninterested in the internal squabbles over the vineyard. But Emma suspected that Isabela knew far more than she let on. And, according to a recent tip, Victor had been working on a secret business deal with a foreign investor in the months leading up to his death. A deal that could explain not only the financial strain the vineyard was under but possibly the motive for his murder.

Emma arrived at the Castello estate just before dusk. The sprawling villa, with its grand arches and terraced gardens, seemed almost untouched by the chaos unravelling inside. But Emma could sense the tension lingering beneath the surface, even in the quiet moments. She was ushered into the drawing room, where Isabela sat by the large window, a glass of wine in her hand. Her back was straight, her posture elegant, as though nothing in the world could disturb her calm exterior.

"Detective Cross," Isabela greeted, her voice smooth and controlled. "I assume you have more questions."

Emma didn't waste time with pleasantries. "Yes, I do, Isabela. I need to know more about Victor's dealings before his death, particularly a business deal he was negotiating with a foreign investor."

Isabela's expression remained impassive, but Emma noticed a slight tightening around her eyes. "I don't know what you're referring to, Detective. Victor handled the vineyard's business. I wasn't involved."

Emma raised an eyebrow, her tone steady but firm. "I find that hard to believe. You've always had influence over the vineyard's affairs, Isabela. Even if Victor kept some things from you, this deal was too significant for you not to know about. I'm asking you to be honest with me—because this deal may be directly tied to his death."

Isabela took a slow sip of her wine, her eyes never leaving Emma's. For a moment, the room was filled with an uncomfortable silence. Then, finally, Isabela set her glass down and sighed.

"I suppose there's no point in hiding it any longer," she said softly, her voice tinged with something like regret. "Yes, there was a deal. Victor had been negotiating with a foreign investor for several months. It was supposed to be a lifeline for the vineyard."

Emma leaned in slightly, her pulse quickening. "A lifeline? What do you mean?"

Isabela's gaze turned toward the window, her eyes distant. "The vineyard was in trouble, more trouble than anyone knew. Victor had overextended himself financially—between the costs of producing his final vintage, the pressure from his illegal dealings, and the land disputes, the vineyard was on the verge of collapse. He was desperate."

Emma's mind raced. This was the first time anyone had openly acknowledged just how dire the vineyard's financial situation had become. "So Victor was trying to sell part of the vineyard? Or was it something more?"

Isabela shook her head. "No, he wasn't selling the vineyard. He was trying to secure funding—an infusion of cash to keep everything afloat. But it wasn't just about money. This investor, a man named Sergei

Ivanov, had connections in markets Victor wanted to break into. The deal would have opened up new international distribution channels, made Castello wines available to an elite clientele overseas."

Emma frowned. "And how did Victor know Ivanov? What kind of man was he?"

Isabela hesitated, her fingers tightening around the stem of her wine glass. "Ivanov wasn't... reputable. He had a reputation for operating in the grey areas of the law. Victor knew it was risky, but he felt like he had no choice. The vineyard needed the money, and Ivanov was offering a way out."

Emma's heart sank. This was exactly the kind of deal that could lead to dangerous consequences. "And what were the terms of the deal? Was Victor going to partner with Ivanov long-term?"

Isabela's face darkened. "That's where things started to unravel. Ivanov's terms were harsh. He wanted a controlling interest in the vineyard's international operations. Victor agreed, but only because he believed he could renegotiate once the initial deal went through. But Ivanov wasn't a man you could outmanoeuvre. Victor realized too late that he was being cornered."

Emma's mind raced, piecing the puzzle together. If Victor had gotten in too deep with Ivanov, it could explain the mounting pressure in the months before his death. And if Ivanov was a man with questionable morals, he might have taken drastic measures to ensure that Victor didn't back out of the deal.

"Did anyone else know about this deal?" Emma asked carefully. "Marco? Alessandro? Adriana?"

Isabela's expression remained unreadable, but her voice softened. "I don't think so. Victor kept the details of the deal very close to his chest. He didn't trust anyone with it—not even me, not really. But I knew he was scared. He wouldn't admit it, but I could see the fear in his eyes. He knew he was in over his head."

Emma nodded, her mind spinning with the implications. "Do you think Ivanov had something to do with Victor's death?"

Isabela's gaze sharpened, and for the first time, her calm exterior seemed to crack. "I don't know. But I wouldn't put it past him. Ivanov is a ruthless man, Detective. If Victor tried to back out of the deal, or if he failed to deliver on his promises, Ivanov wouldn't have hesitated to eliminate the problem."

Emma's heart pounded. A foreign investor with ties to illegal markets, a desperate Victor Castello trying to save his crumbling empire, and a deal that could have destroyed everything—this was a powerful motive. If Ivanov had seen Victor as a liability, then Victor's death might not have been about family rivalry or vineyard politics. It might have been a calculated move to protect a business interest.

"Where is Ivanov now?" Emma asked, her voice tight.

Isabela shook her head. "I don't know. After Victor's death, I stopped hearing from him. But if you're right, Detective—if he had something to do with this—then he's not going to be easy to find."

Emma stood, the weight of the new information settling heavily on her shoulders. Victor had been playing a dangerous game, and it had cost him his life. Now, Emma needed to track down Sergei Ivanov and find out what role he had played in Victor's murder.

"Thank you for your honesty, Isabela," Emma said quietly. "I'll do everything I can to get to the bottom of this."

As she turned to leave, Isabela's voice stopped her.

"Detective," she said softly, her eyes haunted. "Be careful. Ivanov isn't like the others. He's dangerous."

Emma nodded, her determination hardening. "I know. But I won't stop until I get answers."

As Emma left the Castello estate, the cool evening air filling her lungs, she knew that the investigation was reaching its most dangerous phase. Victor's murder had always been about more than just family rivalries—it had been about power, control, and the high-stakes world of international business.

And now, with Sergei Ivanov in the picture, Emma realized that the game was far more deadly than she had ever imagined.

The Castello vineyard's legacy was tainted.

And the final answers were still hidden, waiting to be uncovered.

Chapter 28: The Rossi Deception

Detective Emma Cross had thought she was beginning to untangle the web of deceit surrounding Victor Castello's murder. Between the family's bitter rivalries, hidden business deals, and Victor's dangerous connections, she had unearthed more secrets than she ever anticipated. But nothing could have prepared her for the bombshell she was about to uncover—a twist that would shake everything she thought she knew about the case.

Luca Rossi and Victor Castello—rivals for generations, sworn enemies in both business and family. Emma had always believed their feud was genuine, fuelled by long-standing grudges and deep-rooted animosity. But as she dug deeper into Victor's financial records and business dealings, she stumbled upon something that shattered the illusion of their rivalry.

Victor Castello and Luca Rossi had been working together. In secret.

It all started when Emma received an unexpected call from one of the vineyard's accountants, a man who had quietly been investigating irregularities in the books. He was reluctant to speak at first, but eventually, the pressure of the ongoing investigation had been too much for him. He invited Emma to meet him at a quiet café in the village, where he handed over a stack of documents.

"These are the financial records from both the Castello and Rossi vineyards," the accountant explained nervously. "I don't think anyone was supposed to see this. But I couldn't keep it to myself anymore."

Emma thumbed through the papers, her brow furrowing as she began to understand what she was looking at. The records showed a series of unusual transactions between Victor and Luca—large sums of money being transferred back and forth, seemingly disguised as legitimate business expenses. But it was more than just financial exchanges. The two men had been manipulating the wine market together, driving up the prices of their respective vintages while controlling distribution channels in the region.

Victor Castello and Luca Rossi, lifelong rivals, had been conspiring in secret to dominate the wine industry—and profiting handsomely from it.

Emma's pulse quickened as she realized the gravity of what she had uncovered. The bitter feud between the Castello and Rossi families had been nothing more than a facade, a public rivalry designed to distract everyone from the real power play happening behind the scenes. By manipulating prices and controlling the market, Victor and Luca had ensured that both of their vineyards remained at the top, while competitors struggled to keep up.

But why had they kept it a secret? And more importantly, what had gone wrong between them?

With the financial documents in hand, Emma knew she had to confront Luca Rossi. The truth was out, and she needed to know how far Luca's involvement had gone—and whether it had led to Victor's death.

Emma arrived at the Rossi estate later that afternoon. The sprawling vineyard was eerily quiet, the rows of vines stretching out toward the horizon under the fading light. Luca had agreed to meet with her, though Emma could sense his wariness over the phone. He had always maintained his innocence, claiming that the feud with Victor was real, that their business rivalry had been cutthroat for years. But now, Emma had the proof that it was all a lie.

Luca met her in the main hall of the Rossi villa, his expression guarded as he offered her a seat.

"You said you had something important to discuss, Detective," Luca began, his voice cool. "I assume it's about Victor's death."

Emma didn't waste any time. She placed the stack of documents on the table between them and slid them toward Luca.

"It's about more than Victor's death, Luca," she said, her tone firm. "It's about the truth. The truth that you and Victor were in business together, secretly manipulating wine prices and controlling the market."

Luca's face remained expressionless, but Emma saw the flicker of surprise in his eyes. He hesitated for a moment, glancing down at the papers before meeting her gaze again.

"So, you found out," Luca said quietly, his voice steady but lacking the usual bravado. "I suppose it was only a matter of time."

Emma leaned forward, her eyes locked on Luca's. "You've been lying to everyone—your family, the Castellos, the entire wine industry. All this time, you and Victor were working together to deceive people, to make yourselves even more powerful. Why, Luca? Why keep it a secret?"

Luca sighed, his shoulders sagging slightly as he seemed to accept that the truth could no longer be hidden. "It wasn't just about power, Detective. It was about survival. Victor and I—our families have been at each other's throats for generations. The rivalry was real, but the business landscape changed. The wine industry became more competitive, and we both knew that if we didn't adapt, we'd be crushed by the competition."

"So you decided to team up," Emma said, her voice cold. "You pretended to be enemies while working together behind the scenes. You manipulated the market to keep your vineyards at the top."

Luca nodded slowly. "Yes. We saw an opportunity and took it. By controlling prices and distribution, we could dictate the terms of the industry. No one suspected a thing, because everyone believed we hated each other. It was the perfect cover."

Emma's mind raced. The conspiracy between Luca and Victor explained so much—why the two men had remained at the top of the wine industry for so long, despite the fierce competition. But it also raised new questions.

"Why keep it a secret from your families?" Emma asked, her voice sharp. "Why not bring Marco, Alessandro, or Adriana into the plan? Surely they could have helped."

Luca's expression darkened. "Victor didn't trust his children. He thought they were too focused on their own ambitions to see the bigger picture. And as for me—well, my own family had their doubts about my leadership. Victor and I agreed it was better to keep things between us. Fewer loose ends that way."

Emma narrowed her eyes. "But something went wrong, didn't it? What happened between you and Victor? Why did the deal fall apart?"

Luca's jaw tightened, and for the first time, Emma saw a flash of anger in his eyes. "Victor got greedy. He started making moves without telling me—trying to cut me out of certain deals, working on his final vintage as if it would be his legacy alone. I confronted him about it, but he brushed me off, said I was being paranoid. He was planning to take everything for himself."

Emma's heart pounded as she began to understand. "So you killed him."

Luca's eyes blazed with indignation. "No! I didn't kill Victor, Detective. Yes, we were partners, and yes, things between us had become strained. But I had no reason to kill him. I wanted to resolve our differences, not end his life."

Emma studied him, weighing his words carefully. Luca had every reason to be angry with Victor, especially if Victor had been trying to cut him out of the business. But had that anger been enough to drive Luca to murder?

"You had motive, Luca," Emma said quietly. "If Victor had cut you out of the deals, if he had threatened your control over the market, you would have lost everything. You had every reason to want him dead."

Luca's face twisted with frustration. "You don't understand. I didn't want him dead. I wanted to make things right. Victor's murder—it wasn't about the business. It was something else. Something darker."

Emma felt a chill run down her spine. "What do you mean?"

Luca leaned forward, his voice low and urgent. "Victor was involved in things I didn't even know about—things far more dangerous than our price-fixing scheme. I started hearing whispers, rumours about his connections to foreign investors, about deals that had nothing to do with wine. I think he was in over his head, and someone else wanted him dead. Someone powerful."

Emma's mind raced as she remembered Isabela's revelation about Sergei Ivanov, the foreign investor Victor had been dealing with. Could Ivanov have been the one to orchestrate Victor's murder?

"Whoever killed Victor," Luca said softly, "they're not done yet. The game's still being played, and the stakes are higher than you think."

Emma stood, her heart pounding with the weight of what she had just learned. The conspiracy between Luca and Victor had been dangerous, but it was only part of the larger picture. Victor's death wasn't just about greed or family rivalries—it was about power, control, and the dark forces lurking beneath the surface of the wine industry.

As Emma left the Rossi estate, she knew that the real battle for the vineyard's future was just beginning.

And the Rossi deception was only the first move in a much larger game.

Chapter 29: Stained Hands

The vineyard sprawled before Detective Emma Cross like a maze of secrets, each row of vines hiding a potential clue, a whisper of the truth about Victor Castello's murder. The more she uncovered, the clearer it became that this case wasn't just about family betrayal or financial greed—it was about deception on a grand scale, and the stakes were far higher than she'd ever imagined. Now, she had another thread to pull: a vineyard worker who had been paid off to cover up a key piece of evidence.

It was an anonymous tip, like so many others she'd received during the investigation, that had led her to this latest revelation. The message was brief, but its implications were enormous: One of the workers was paid to hide something from you. Check the southern fields.

Emma didn't waste time. She drove out to the southern fields of Castello Vineyards, where the workers were busy pruning the last of the vines before the harvest season ended. It was a quieter part of the vineyard, far from the estate's main building, where few people ventured unless they had business among the vines. It was the perfect place for something—or someone—to disappear unnoticed.

As she approached, she spotted a worker leaning against a fence post, wiping sweat from his brow. His name was Roberto, and Emma recognized him from her earlier visits to the vineyard. He had been cooperative during her initial interviews, but something about him had always seemed off—too nervous, too eager to please. Now, Emma wondered if he had more to hide than she initially thought.

Emma made her way over to him, her footsteps crunching on the dry dirt. Roberto looked up as she approached, his eyes narrowing slightly, though he tried to hide his unease behind a polite nod.

"Detective Cross," Roberto greeted, his voice steady, but his eyes betrayed a flicker of anxiety. "What brings you out here?"

Emma didn't waste time. "I need to talk to you, Roberto. I've received information that suggests you may have been paid off to cover something up. Something important. I'm giving you one chance to tell me the truth."

Roberto's face paled slightly, and he shifted uncomfortably, glancing around as if hoping no one else was watching. He swallowed hard, then gave a nervous chuckle. "I don't know what you're talking about, Detective. I've just been doing my job."

Emma stepped closer, her gaze sharp and unyielding. "This isn't the time to lie, Roberto. I know someone paid you to keep quiet about something—something related to Victor Castello's murder. If you don't tell me the truth now, I'll make sure you're implicated in the cover-up. Do you really want that on your hands?"

Roberto's facade of calm crumbled. He glanced around nervously again, then lowered his voice to a whisper. "You don't understand, Detective. I didn't want to be involved in this. I was just trying to protect my family."

Emma's pulse quickened. She was getting closer to the truth. "Involved in what? Tell me everything."

Roberto hesitated, wiping his hands on his shirt as if trying to rid himself of an invisible stain. He looked at Emma, desperation in his eyes. "It wasn't supposed to be like this. I didn't know what they were planning. I was just doing my job, helping with the harvest, when… I found something. Something I shouldn't have seen."

Emma's heart pounded. "What did you find?"

Roberto glanced around again, then spoke in a low, hurried voice. "It was a few days before Victor's death. I was working in the cellar, helping to move the barrels for the final vintage. But one of the barrels—something was wrong with it. The wine inside wasn't right. It smelled… off. Like it had been tampered with."

Emma's mind raced. The final vintage. The one Victor had been so obsessed with—the one that had been sabotaged. "What did you do?"

"I tried to tell the foreman," Roberto continued, his voice trembling. "But before I could, someone else came to me. A man I didn't recognize. He told me to forget about it, said it wasn't my concern. He offered me money—a lot of money—to keep my mouth shut and not ask any questions."

Emma's stomach churned. "Did you take the money?"

Roberto nodded slowly, shame flooding his face. "I didn't know what else to do. My family needs the money, and he made it sound like it wasn't a big deal. Just a small problem with the batch, nothing serious. I thought... I thought if I just kept quiet, it would all blow over."

"But it didn't," Emma said, her voice firm. "Victor was killed, and that wine was likely part of the reason."

Roberto swallowed hard, his face paling further. "I didn't know. I didn't know they were going to kill him. I thought it was just about the wine, that it would be fixed before the harvest."

Emma took a deep breath, her mind racing. The tampering with the final vintage, the payments to keep it quiet—it was all part of the larger conspiracy. But who was behind it? Who had paid Roberto to keep silent, and why had they been so desperate to cover it up?

"Who paid you?" Emma asked, her voice sharp. "I need a name."

Roberto hesitated again, his eyes darting toward the vineyard as if he expected someone to be watching. Finally, he spoke, his voice barely a whisper. "I don't know his name. But he wasn't from the vineyard. I've seen him once or twice, always in the shadows, talking to some of the other workers. I think he's connected to whoever Victor was dealing with—the foreign investors."

Emma's heart skipped a beat. The foreign investor. Sergei Ivanov. The pieces were beginning to fall into place. Ivanov had been pressuring Victor about the deal, and now it seemed he—or someone working for him—had tampered with the final vintage and paid off workers like Roberto to cover it up.

"Where did you last see this man?" Emma pressed.

Roberto shook his head. "I haven't seen him since Victor's death. But I heard whispers that he's still around, keeping an eye on things. People are scared, Detective. They know something bigger is going on, but no one wants to get involved."

Emma stood silently for a moment, piecing together the information. Ivanov—or someone tied to him—had orchestrated the tampering of the vintage and had been willing to bribe workers to cover it up. This wasn't just about ruining the final vintage; it was about exerting control, manipulating Victor, and possibly eliminating him when things got too complicated.

"Thank you for your honesty, Roberto," Emma said quietly. "But this isn't over yet. I need you to stay quiet about this until I get to the bottom of it. Do you understand?"

Roberto nodded quickly, relief washing over his face. "I won't say a word, Detective. I swear."

Emma gave him a curt nod and turned to leave, her mind racing with the weight of this new information. The cover-up had reached deep into the heart of the vineyard, and now she was certain that the key to Victor's murder was tied to his dealings with Ivanov.

As Emma walked through the vineyard, the cool evening air brushing against her skin, she knew that the final pieces of the puzzle were coming together. But whoever was behind this had already killed once to protect their secret.

And Emma wasn't about to let them get away with it.

The Castello vineyard was stained with blood and deceit.

And Emma was determined to expose the truth, no matter the cost.

Part 6: The Final Pour
Chapter 30: The Killer Revealed

The vineyard stretched out in front of Detective Emma Cross like an endless sea of vines, their roots tangled deep in the soil, just as the secrets of the Castello family were knotted in betrayal and jealousy. After weeks of investigation, unearthing hidden business deals, shattered dreams, and twisted family ties, Emma knew she was on the cusp of revealing the truth. The final pieces of the puzzle were in place, and it was time to reveal Victor Castello's killer.

Emma had gathered the Castello family in the grand dining room of the estate, the very place where they had once come together to celebrate their legacy. But tonight, the room was thick with tension. The once-proud heirs of Castello Vineyards—Marco, Alessandro, Adriana—and their mother, Isabela, sat around the table, their faces strained, their eyes flickering with suspicion and fear. They knew that the truth was about to be uncovered, and none of them could escape the consequences.

Emma stood at the head of the table, the weight of the moment settling over her. She took a deep breath and began.

"I've spent the last few weeks investigating Victor Castello's murder, and I've uncovered more than just one man's death," Emma said, her voice calm but firm. "I've uncovered the lies that have defined this family for years—secrets about your father's business dealings, his plans to sell the vineyard, and the betrayal that ultimately led to his death."

The room was silent, the family members watching her with a mixture of dread and curiosity. Emma's gaze moved from one face to the next before continuing.

"Victor's death wasn't just a random act of violence. It was the result of years of jealousy, manipulation, and the fight for control of this vineyard. Each of you had a reason to want him out of the way. Marco, you believed you were the rightful heir, but your father never trusted you to run the vineyard. Alessandro, you resented your brother and wanted to prove yourself as the true leader. And Adriana, you were passed over time and time again, despite your ambition to take control of the family business."

Adriana's face flushed with anger, but she said nothing.

Emma turned to Isabela. "And you, Isabela, had the most to lose. You knew about Victor's plan to sell the vineyard. You realized that if he went through with it, your family's legacy would be destroyed. You manipulated your children into helping you, but you never intended for things to go this far."

Isabela's eyes darkened, her lips pressed into a thin line. She knew what was coming, but she remained silent, her calm exterior cracking only slightly.

Emma stepped closer to the table, her voice growing sharper. "But the murder wasn't just about stopping the sale of the vineyard. It was about something more personal. It was about betrayal."

She turned her gaze to Marco, whose face had grown pale. "Marco, you were the one who killed your father."

A collective gasp echoed through the room, but Marco's face remained frozen in shock. His lips parted as if to protest, but no words came out.

"You were desperate to prove yourself to your father," Emma continued, her eyes never leaving his. "You thought that by getting rid of him, you could finally take control of the vineyard, make it your own. But it wasn't just about the vineyard, was it? It was about the betrayal you felt when you realized your father was going to sell everything—cutting you, Alessandro, and Adriana out of the family's future."

Marco's hands trembled as he gripped the edge of the table, his face a mixture of fury and disbelief. "That's not true!" he shouted, his voice cracking. "I didn't kill him! I wanted to save the vineyard, not destroy it!"

Emma's voice softened, but her words were unyielding. "You didn't plan to kill him, Marco. But in the heat of the moment, when you confronted him, something snapped. You saw him as the enemy—someone who had betrayed you and the family, someone who was about to destroy everything you'd ever known."

Marco shook his head, tears filling his eyes. "I didn't mean to... I just wanted him to stop."

Emma nodded slowly, her heart heavy with the weight of the truth. "But he didn't stop, did he? He refused to back down, and in that moment, you struck him. It was impulsive, driven by anger and betrayal. But that's what killed him."

Adriana stood abruptly, her face pale with shock. "Marco? You did this?"

Marco buried his face in his hands, his shoulders shaking with guilt. "I didn't mean for it to happen like this," he choked out, his voice barely audible. "I just wanted him to see that he was wrong... but he wouldn't listen."

Alessandro's face twisted with anger as he looked at his brother. "You killed him because you couldn't handle the truth! You let your jealousy destroy this family!"

Isabela, who had remained silent until now, finally spoke, her voice trembling with a mixture of rage and sorrow. "You've destroyed everything, Marco. Everything we fought for. Your father... your father may have been wrong, but you had no right to take his life."

Marco's head hung low, his tears falling onto the table as the weight of his actions finally crashed down on him.

Emma stepped back, allowing the family to absorb the devastating truth. Victor Castello's death had not been a calculated assassination or a cold-blooded murder. It had been the result of a son's desperation and anger, born out of years of betrayal and jealousy.

But the family's hands were far from clean. Isabela had pushed her children to the edge, manipulating their emotions and feeding their insecurities. Marco had taken the final step, but they had all played a part in the tragedy that had unfolded.

The Castello legacy, once a source of pride and power, was now stained with blood.

As Emma prepared to leave the estate, she offered them one final thought. "Victor's murder may have been an impulsive act, but the fractures in this family have been there for years. You've been fighting for control of a vineyard that was never yours to control. And now, because of that, you've lost everything."

The vineyard, once a symbol of wealth and prestige, now stood as a reminder of the greed, betrayal, and broken dreams that had destroyed the Castello name.

And in the end, the legacy they had fought so hard to protect had been lost—forever tainted by the blood of the man who had built it.

Chapter 31: The Last Glass

The Castello vineyard was quiet in the aftermath of the revelations that had torn the family apart. Once a symbol of wealth, prestige, and tradition, it now stood as a monument to shattered dreams and betrayal. Detective Emma Cross had uncovered the truth behind Victor Castello's murder, exposing a family conspiracy and the bitter emotions that had led his eldest son, Marco, to kill him in a moment of rage. But now, as the dust settled, the question that remained was: What would become of Castello Vineyards?

Emma watched from the edge of the vineyard as the setting sun cast a golden glow over the rows of vines, the once-immaculate estate now marred by the knowledge of what had transpired within its walls. The Castello family had gathered for one final meeting, a moment to decide the vineyard's future—a future that had once seemed certain but now hung by a fragile thread.

Inside the grand dining room of the estate, Marco, Alessandro, Adriana, and Isabela sat around the same table where the truth had been revealed just days earlier. Their faces were haggard, worn by the weight of their father's death and the knowledge that their legacy had been tainted forever. Emma had chosen to stay on the estate for a few more days, knowing that the aftermath of her investigation was far from over. The family's dynamics had been shattered, and with the vineyard's future on the line, she knew the end of this story would be just as important as solving the murder.

"I don't know what to do anymore," Marco finally said, his voice hoarse and heavy with guilt. He stared down at his hands, which trembled slightly as if the weight of his actions were still pressing down on him. "I didn't mean for any of this to happen."

Alessandro, who had spent much of his life resenting his brother's favoured status, looked at Marco with a mixture of anger and sadness.

"It doesn't matter anymore, Marco. Father is gone, and the vineyard… the vineyard will never be the same."

Adriana, sitting quietly across from them, stared at the untouched glass of wine in front of her. She had always wanted to take control of the vineyard, to prove herself as capable and strong. But now, the dream felt hollow. "We've all lost," she whispered, her voice barely audible. "Everything we thought we were fighting for… it's gone."

Isabela, who had once stood as the matriarch of the family, the orchestrator behind many of the decisions that led to this moment, sat in silence. Her eyes were distant, as if she were mourning not only her husband but also the future she had envisioned for her children. She had wanted to protect the family, to secure their place in the world, but in the end, her manipulations had only deepened the fractures.

The room was heavy with regret, the silence stretching on as each member of the family tried to grapple with the enormity of what had been lost. The vineyard, their inheritance, their identity—everything had been tainted by the blood that had been spilled in the name of control.

Emma stepped forward, breaking the silence. "The vineyard is still here," she said quietly, her voice steady but filled with empathy. "The land, the legacy—it's damaged, yes, but not beyond repair. The question now is whether you're willing to pick up the pieces and build something new from the ruins."

Marco looked up, his eyes red-rimmed with grief. "How can we? How can we rebuild after everything that's happened?"

Emma met his gaze, her expression firm but compassionate. "You start by being honest with yourselves and with each other. Victor's legacy wasn't just about the vineyard—it was about the way he controlled all of you. You were all trapped in his expectations, his vision of the future. But now, you have the chance to decide what your legacy will be."

Adriana nodded slowly, understanding what Emma was saying. "We've been so focused on fighting for the vineyard that we lost sight of everything else."

Alessandro sighed, his anger seeming to soften for the first time. "Maybe it's time to let go of the past. Father's way of doing things... it wasn't the only way."

Isabela, her eyes still distant, finally spoke. "Victor wanted this vineyard to be his legacy. But what he failed to realize was that a legacy isn't just about power or wealth. It's about the family that's left behind."

Emma watched as the words sank in, a sense of quiet resolution beginning to settle over the room. The vineyard's future was uncertain, yes, but for the first time, the Castello family seemed willing to confront the truth that had been buried beneath years of secrets and lies.

Marco cleared his throat, his voice steadying. "If we're going to move forward, we need to do it together. No more fighting, no more secrets."

Alessandro nodded in agreement. "Agreed. But we can't rebuild what was. The vineyard has to change."

Adriana looked at her brothers, her determination slowly returning. "Then let's make it something new—something we can be proud of. A vineyard built on honesty, not on Father's manipulations."

Isabela looked at her children, her expression softening as she realized that they were, at last, taking control of their own future. "It won't be easy," she said quietly. "But maybe that's the point. The vineyard's strength comes from the land, not from the lies that have been told over it."

Emma nodded, satisfied that the Castello family had finally come to a crossroads. The vineyard's future would not be determined by Victor's legacy, but by the choices his children made from here on. There would be no more secrets, no more betrayals.

As the family stood up from the table, there was a quiet, unspoken understanding that the past could not be changed, but the future was theirs to shape.

Emma quietly made her way toward the door, her part in the Castello family's story now complete. Before she left, she turned back one final time and spoke.

"You have the vineyard, and you have each other. That's more than enough to build something new. Don't waste it."

With that, Emma stepped out into the night, leaving the Castello family to face the future on their own terms.

Outside, the vineyard stretched on beneath the fading light, the vines still full, still strong. The future of Castello Vineyards hung in the balance, but for the first time, the weight of its past had begun to lift. The family's dreams had been crushed, but perhaps, in the aftermath, something better could grow from the ruins.

The Castello name would live on, but the future of the vineyard now belonged to the children who had fought so hard to inherit it.

The last glass of the old Castello legacy had been poured. Now it was time for the family to decide what came next.

Chapter 32: A New Vintage

The Castello vineyard lay behind her, its sprawling rows of vines disappearing into the twilight as Detective Emma Cross made her way toward the edge of the estate. The air was cool and still, filled with the faint scent of grapes ripening on the vine—grapes that, despite everything, would soon be harvested. Life moved forward, even in the wake of destruction.

Emma paused on a small hill overlooking the vineyard, taking in the view one last time. This case had been more than a murder investigation; it had been an excavation of a family's past—an unearthing of the secrets and betrayals that had shaped the Castello family for generations. Like wine, their lives had been shaped by time, weathered by experience, and marked by the violence that simmered beneath the surface.

Victor Castello had built an empire on those vines, and in doing so, had created a bitter legacy that his family had struggled to inherit. His ambition had driven them, his manipulations had divided them, and ultimately, his death had torn them apart. Yet, in the end, it wasn't Victor's strength or power that would define the future of Castello Vineyards—it was the resilience of the family he had left behind.

As Emma reflected on the events that had led her here, she couldn't help but draw parallels between the family and the vineyard itself. Wine, after all, was a product of its environment, influenced by the soil, the climate, the care—or neglect—it received. The Castello family had been much the same, their lives moulded by their father's control, their ambitions twisted by jealousy and fear. Time had aged them, worn them down, until the pressure had become too much and everything had fractured.

But just as a vineyard could recover after a difficult season, so too could a family—if they were willing to confront the truth and rebuild from the ashes.

Emma knew that the Castello family had a long road ahead of them. Marco would have to live with the knowledge of what he had done, burdened by the guilt of taking his father's life. Alessandro and Adriana would have to find their place in a future that no longer revolved around Victor's approval. And Isabela would have to come to terms with the role she had played in orchestrating the conspiracy that had ultimately destroyed them.

But despite the darkness that had settled over the family, Emma saw glimmers of hope. The vineyard still stood, strong and full of life. The Castello children had agreed to rebuild, to reshape the vineyard in their own image, free from the shadow of their father's legacy. It would take time, and there would be no quick fixes, but they had been given a second chance—one that Victor had denied them for so long.

Emma sighed, the weight of the case finally lifting from her shoulders as she took in the peaceful landscape before her. The vineyard, like the family, had suffered, but it was not beyond saving. If the Castello heirs could learn to work together, to let go of the greed and rivalry that had poisoned them, they could create something new—something better.

In the distance, she could see workers preparing for the next phase of the harvest, their figures silhouetted against the fading light. The grapes would soon be picked, pressed, and turned into wine, beginning the long process of fermentation and aging—a process that, like life itself, required patience, care, and time. And in the end, the result would be something new. A new vintage.

As Emma turned to leave the estate, she thought about the vineyard's future. Castello Vineyards had been built on secrets, but perhaps, in time, it could be reborn in honesty. The scars of the past would never fully fade, but they didn't have to define the future.

The family, like the wine they produced, would have to weather the seasons ahead, each year adding new layers to their story. It wouldn't be easy, but for the first time in years, they had the chance to create something of their own—something that wasn't bound by the sins of the past.

As Emma walked away, the faint glow of the vineyard behind her, she couldn't help but feel a sense of closure. The case was over, but the story of the Castello family wasn't. They had been crushed by their secrets, their lives shaped by time and violence, but now, they had the opportunity to rewrite their future. A new vintage was beginning.

And perhaps, this time, it would be aged to perfection.

Disclaimer:

This is a work of fiction. Names, characters, places, and incidents are either products of the author's imagination or used in a fictitious manner. Any resemblance to actual persons, living or dead, businesses, companies, events, or locales is purely coincidental. The depiction of the wine industry, vineyards, and related practices is based on fictionalized settings and should not be considered an accurate representation of any specific individuals or establishments. The author does not endorse or imply any affiliation with real-world wineries, wine brands, or industry professionals.